I0520101

SWITCHBLADE

TechNoir

Edited by Scotch Rutherford

Switchblade, Special Issue: Tech Noir
First Printing: October 2019

ISBN-13: 978-1-7332976-2-2

©2019 Caledonia Press

www.switchblademag.com

All rights reserved. No part of this journal may be
reproduced or transmitted in any form or by any means
without the prior written permission from the editor or
authors responsible for the images or short fiction
contained herein.

The following stories are works of fiction. All of the names,
characters, organizations, corporations, institutions, events,
and locations portrayed in these works are either products
of the author's imagination, or, if real, used fictitiously. The
resemblance of any character to actual persons (dead or
alive), are purely coincidental.

Stories by the authors: © Eric Beetner, © Callum
McSorley © John Moralee, © Mandi Jourdan, © Hugh
Lessig , © Alec Cizak, © Nick Kolakowski,© Matthew X.
Gomez, © James Edward O'Brien, © Rob D. Smith

Front cover : ©2019 Scotch Rutherford
Back cover : ©2019 Scotch Rutherford

CONTENTS

Welcome to Tech Noir.

It's here. Drone strikes, school shootings, and domestic terrorism. Government tracking, racial profiling. Worldwide surveillance. The eye in the sky sees all, and big brother is watching. The party is still the party, and the only opposition is *the other party*. Newspeak is spoken through a giant mega corporation conglomerate, and theater can never truly be faked. Welcome to the dystopian future they warned us about. The more things change, the more things stay the same—said boomers who never knew anti-hate groups who love to hate anyone outside of the pack, instead of the hate groups whose hatred is the photo negative of the flipside of their inverted doppelganger. War is still the biggest business and funding rebels to destabilize foreign governments is paid off ten-fold in black gold. What *was* edgy is still considered edgy today, by those arm chair revolutionists with sleeved tattoos who push up on yesterday's rebellion from a safe distance. Their time is ripe, but puppets must be trusted, before anyone can pull strings...

Anyone can catch a wave when the tide is coming in. To swim against the current takes courage. And strength. People ask me what side am I on? My side, of course. Call me whatever you like, but don't call yourself a rebel if you don't know free-style. ☠ ☠ ☠ To be a rebel is to stand alone. Just ask Alec Cizak. Quantum computers, and AI are fast approaching at an accelerated clip. You can't fight the future. And even if you could, a revolutionary can only ever be a rebel in his own time. The planet is heating up. The seas are rising. The President of the United States is a reality TV star, and gangsta rap is the new white pop music. Welcome to 2019.

——Scotch Rutherford (Managing Editor)

The Future is Noir

Pulp Modern

Tech Noir Special   Fall 2019

R.Scott '19

Tom Barlow • C.W. Blackwell • Deborah L. Davitt
Angelique Fawns • Nils Gilbertson • J.D. Graves
Zakariah Johnson • Jo Perry • Don Stoll

BROADSWORDS and BLASTERS

Pulp Magazine with Modern Sensibilities

"The Mad Scientists of Modern Pulp"

BROADSWORDS and BLASTERS

Issue 11
Fall 2019

Pulp Magazine with Modern Sensibilities

Stories by
J.C. Pillard
C.J. Casey
E.K. Wagner
Gary Robbe
James Kane
Aaron Emmel
Erica Ruppert
Kevin M. Folliard
Benjamin Chandler

Art by
Luke Spooner

"Goo ... down"

"Ide ... y edited"

"ir"

NEW ISSUE OCTOBER 2019!

Come check us out at
BroadswordsandBlasters.com
and search for us on Amazon.

TOUGH

CRIME STORIES

2

MNEMOPHRENIA

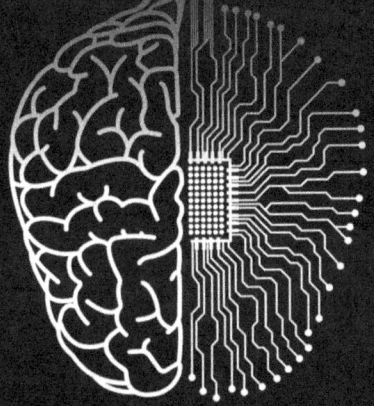

WHAT IS MORE REAL THAN YOUR MEMORIES?

ONE

Stealing memories isn't as easy as it sounds. Okay I don't even know if it sounds easy, but it did to me when Dru explained it.

We work for X-PER VR and our specialty is memory trips, or what the brochure calls "Enhanced lived-in life experiences". The *X-Per* stands for experiences and what it really means is porn. VR tech had been languishing for years. Billions of capital laying fallow in the fields of tech startups and failed app launches. You can watch something through someone else's eyes and it's cool and all, but with the gear on your face, the one-step-removed feeling, people rarely went back to it. Then some genius in Korea figured out how to harvest actual memories and share them. That way, if you want to climb a mountain but don't have the skills, you can literally live someone else's memory of it and not only see it, but *feel* it. You *are* there.

People were interested. And we're humans so it took us all of about ten seconds to figure out that we could pull memories of having sex with incredibly hot women and let creeps and trolls experience *exactly* what that was like with an implanted memory.

A memory I immediately wipe the second their allotted time they paid for is over. You don't get to keep the memories. That's how we get them coming back.

Like most apps and tech stuff going back to the VHS tape, porn was the killer app that put it over the top and turned it into a multi-billion dollar industry.

We had a stable of guys who let us harvest their memories, willing women ready to take a payday to let the memory be "made" if you know what I mean. And more than enough sad, lonely dudes eager to fork over cash for a real dopamine and serotonin rush with a real orgasm from the sessions. You were there, man, doin' it to that chick and your brain didn't know that you were really laying in a reclining chair for $300 an hour.

So when Dru had his idea, we all thought it was great. X-Per had been an early adopter and had been one of the top experience companies. Now companies were schilling memories on every corner, it seemed. We needed a new angle.

"Hot chicks are one thing," Dru said. "What we need are, like, real celebrities. Actors and singers and shit."

"Something tells me they don't need the cash," I said. "There's no way they'd sell us their memories."

"So we don't ask them."

"What the hell does that mean?"

"We take them."

"Steal someone's memories?"

"Yeah, why not?"

Shit. Yeah, why not?

*

It's not all that hard to figure out who's screwing a celebrity. And the extraction had been honed down from the drill-a-hole in the skull version from the original Korean development, to a non-invasive five minute procedure. One that you would still notice when the probe went into your nasal cavity to find its way into your frontal lobe. So, we had to knock someone out in order to extract any fresh memories.

And freshness was key.

For years now they've been peddling some lame, half-remembered bullshit like old Super Bowls and World Series. A lot of it featured black spots where bits have been forgotten. Then if the person went to the bathroom or something, all that's in there. The trend lately has been curated experiences. Someone will go hang gliding or skydiving, then land and go right into extraction. Get 'em while they're fresh like little memory muffins.

The sex stuff, too. We have our studio where our volunteers come in, do the deed, then get extracted. We do the women too, but surprise, surprise—about 95% of our clients for the porn stuff are guys.

So Dru's plan was to find out who was dating some hot young thing, find out where they live, then go get them and hope they had a fresh memory we could sell under the table to clients willing to pay bigger bucks to have sex with someone famous.

Sure, it sounds stupid now. We went for it at the time, especially since we had more and more time to talk about since the chairs were less and less booked up with clients.

TWO

One day, Dru comes in and says, "The guy from that show is banging Lindy Shaw."

"Guy from what show?"

"I don't know, the historical one where they all live in the nineteen eighties. With all the crazy outfits and shit. And the phones have cords."

"Oh yeah."

"The important part is the Lindy Shaw part. How much would guys pay to get with her?"

9

The biggest pop singing star of the moment? A lot. They would pay a whole hell of a lot. Lindy had been a hitmaker for over a year now, just turned eighteen. Probably had about six months left on her celebrity before the world threw her over for someone else, but if we could get that memory…

Dru held up his tablet. "I found where they live."

A map beckoned on his screen. Not too far away.

"They live together?" I asked.

"Yeah. She owns it. He's got, like, a small part on that show. And she's got fifty million in the bank."

"Think we can get in? There's probably security."

"They might have security, but I have my cousin Alistair."

I could only guess that was a good thing.

*

Up into the Hollywood Hills I went with Dru and his cousin. Back behind a high fence I had to give it to Alistair, he really did know his shit. He got us in and past the alarm with no problem. Dru carried the extraction probe, I carried the knockout gas. We used a new synthetic that would take people out for thirty minutes almost to the second. Take the little grape-size balls and crack them open, put them into the vaporizer and let the client inhale. About five seconds later, they're out. We didn't have a vaporizer so I brought two capsules and the plan was to crack them open and shove them into the room with Lindy and her man.

The house was something else. Definitely like the house of a rich girl who was still in her teens.

A combo of hired decorator flourishes with teen pop star sloppiness and primary colors.

It was two thirty five in the morning. Hard to tell with a famous person like that if they'd still be out at the clubs, but we got lucky and no one seemed to be awake. The only question mark now was whether or not they'd had sex that night. Given the way these two hot young things looked, I sure as hell hoped so. It would be a shame to let all that hotness go to waste.

We found the bedroom. I handed out face masks with re-breathers, slid one on myself and then cracked the two capsules and pushed them under the door. I counted to thirty then we went in.

The bedroom was a mess. Guess the maid was off that day. The bed itself looked appropriately disheveled for them to have had sex. From the looks of things, it had been wild. Actor boy was shirtless and splayed out across the bed, which was freakin' huge by the way. There's a King bed but this was more like an Emperor or something. Then little Lindy Shaw. She was tiny in person. Also shirtless. A hundred million guys in America had probably gone to bed wondering what she looked like topless, and there I was looking right at it. I noticed cousin Alistair looking a little too long at her. I snapped my fingers once at him. Even behind the mask I could see a look of shame on his face. Didn't stop him from going back and staring at her chest the second he was done looking contrite at me.

Dru was all business. He crouched over the actor boy and flicked on the headlamp he wore. The bright light shone as he guided the probe up the actor's nose and into position. With eyes on the readout screen for signs of recent memory

11

activity, Dru was able to zero in on brain activity from the last six hours. He'd brought a twenty terabyte chip to store data on, not knowing exactly how far we'd have to go back into his memories. There'd be a lot to sort through back at the lab, but the payday would be worth it.

I turned around to see Alistair about to clamp a sweaty hand around one of Lindy's tits.

"Hey."

He froze.

"The fuck you doing?"

"What?" he said. "She's out. She won't know."

"Don't be a fuckin' sleaze."

"You're stealing this guy's brain waves to know what it's like to fuck her. What's the difference?"

"I'm not really touching her. It's different. So knock it off."

Alistair puffed up like he had some moral leg to stand on. "You guys ain't paying me enough to keep me from taking a little side bonus."

Dru didn't take his eyes off the task, but spoke up with, "Alistair, stand down. Go check the alarms again."

"There's no silent alarm. I told you."

"Go check it again."

Like a bratty child, he huffed once and left the room.

"Sorry about that," Dru said.

"Hard to draw a line like that with criminals, I guess."

Criminals. Man, that's what we were. Who the hell was I to be telling anyone about right and wrong?

THREE

12

We got back to the lab and Dru uploaded the file. Memories transfer roughly in real time so after five hours of waiting, sleeping and eating shit food we had about six hours of memories from the actor dude. Dru sat down to scrub the footage and see if we'd struck gold.

On our monitor systems we could scroll through the timeline without implanting anything. That way we just watched, we didn't *experience*. But I tell you what, I knew Dru would be the first to strap in and try it out if we came across these two pretties having sex.

We'd dropped his cousin off on the way back and I was glad about that. That guy creeped me out. But I guess that's the kind of guy you call when you need to break in to someone's house. He did us right, at least.

I was still tired as hell so stayed laid out while Dru watched. After about twenty minutes of high speed scrolling he called me over.

"Hey, hey check this out. Here we go."

I sat up and looked over Dru's shoulder. The view from actor boy's eyes was a club, pulsing between dark and light with the strobes and a mirrorball. Lindy was in front of him talking to a fan.

Dru picked up one ear of his headphones when he spoke to me. "This chick is a massive fan and there's serious vibe going on right now."

I found a chair and slid in next to Dru. I didn't judge people. I get it. The voyeur aspect of this shit was pretty enticing.

Dru scrubbed forward. The young fan, a caramel-colored girl who was short and thin and really sexy, kept laughing at everything Lindy said and kept touching her arm. Now and then Dru would stop and play for a little bit so he could

13

hear what they were saying. He stopped his fast forward and played and right where he stopped the fangirl leaned in and kissed Lindy on the mouth. Dru turned to me with a giant grin on his face.

"Holy shit, dude. If we get her with another chick, or fuck, a three-way. Do you know how much we could charge for that?"

I didn't know, but I could imagine it.

Dru went into overdrive while I dreamed of money transfers going into our accounts. Dru skipped ahead to when they were back at Lindy's place. The young fan had come home with them. She and Lindy had been kissing, she and the actor boy had been kissing. This was better than I'd hoped for the first outing.

They took the girl into a room, but not the bedroom. I hadn't seen any more than the bedroom and hallway when we were there so I had no idea where they were in the house. Recording studio maybe? This fangirl wanted to show Lindy some song she wrote?

"Dude," Dru said. "Dude!"

He slapped my arm but didn't take his eyes off the screen. I kinda wished I also had headphones, but I damn well was going to get implanted right after Dru did to see what this was like. I'd never been with two girls before. Dru was excited about the next turn of events. They tied fangirl up. The room wasn't a studio. It was some kind of sex playroom. Rubber floors, straps and tie-downs. Kinky shit. Maybe not for every taste, but for the people who would pay top dollar for it, this was in the next price range.

"The fuck…?"

Dru leaned in closer to the screen. The actor boy didn't always give us the clearest view

14

through his eyes, so when he turned to show Lindy and she was naked, there was a moment of pleasant shock. She'd undressed out of his view, but the thing that shocked us both was the knife in her hand.

By the look on the fangirl's face, she was shocked as well. By then she had a soft silk gag in her mouth. But this soft core kink fest was about to get hardcore. Dru reached out and clamped his hand on my forearm when Lindy stepped up and slashed the girl across the throat. She turned to actor boy with a huge smile on her face and blood spatters across her cheeks.

Lindy Shaw, pop idol to millions, turned again and started hacking at this girl until the little caramel-colored body was in ribbons.

Dru turned off the feed. He stood up and threw off the headphones.

"What the fuck was that?"

"I don't know, man," I said.

"She just killed that chick."

I nodded. Thank fuck we didn't implant that. Once you feel that, you could never unfeel it, y'know?

"That's fucked up."

"Yeah."

"She's a killer."

"Yeah."

FOUR

We didn't say anything for about twenty minutes. The screen sat black, neither one of us wanted to turn it back on and see what happened next.

"Maybe it was fake," I said.

"Fake for who? Why would it be fake?"

I had no answer.

Dru stood and let out a deep sigh, like he was trying expel the image of seeing what we'd seen.

"Okay, this is majorly fucked up, but hear me out."

"Hear what out?"

Dru looked pained by what he was saying. "People would pay a shit-ton of money to see them screwing, right?"

"Yeah."

"Well, you know there are some sick fucks out there who would pay millions, serious millions, to get implanted with a murder. They'd get to do it, but not do it, y'know?"

"Yeah. I know how our fucking business works, Dru. But we're not gonna sell a murder memory."

"But people would totally pay for it, right?"

"It's not even her memory."

"Right, right. We'd have to go back and get it from her."

"Will you stop. We have to destroy this file. Delete it and wipe the drive."

"Yeah. Totally. You're right."

I wanted to get as far away as I could from the new reality of what we'd found, so we shut down the system and left.

*

I went home and got some sleep, trying to shake off what I'd seen. That's the thing about dealing in memories, you realize both how fragile they are and how easily lost, but also how indelible they are once they stick in your skull. Got a mole you don't want? Laser it off. Born with an extra pinky finger? Cut that shit off. Memory you don't want anymore? You're fucked. It's with you for life, never more than a few inches under

16

the surface like some lurking shark ready to break the surface and seriously fuck up your day.

Rich people have always been weird, right? You get to a point and you've got everything you ever wanted by age seventeen and where do you go from there? Thrill killing is where, I guess.

Damn, this world. We hit twelve billion people and then we managed to snuff out more than a billion of those after the water rose here, dried out there and was poisoned almost everywhere. But we're resilient, us humans. And as soon as we're complacent again, what do we do? Kill each other for fun.

I got to work late the next day and I didn't know if Dru would be pushing to find a new celebrity couple to harvest memories from or if he had some different plan to make us rich. Please help me if I ever get so rich I think a fun night out is slicing a girl into spaghetti.

I found Dru hunched over his monitor, headphones on and a fingernail in his teeth. I tapped his shoulder and he jumped about a foot.

He threw off his headphones. "Dude, what the...?"

"Relax, man. I was just saying hi."

"Well don't sneak up on a guy."

I tried to see what was on his monitor. The room looked familiar. So did the blood.

"Are you...? Dammit, don't watch that shit again."

"This is different," he said. His face was a nine year old boy being scolded by his parents. Guilt, and shame.

"What do you mean?"

"This is...she's messed up, man."

"Who is?" I knew, though.

"We went back." I didn't say anything. I could tell he wanted to spill it. I wasn't so sure I wanted to hear it. "Me and Alistair. We went back to get more from him."

I checked around us to make sure nobody was listening. The other employees worked outside of the lab so we were alone. I found a chair and slumped down.

"I got some from her, too."

I could tell he hadn't slept. Not hard to do with the chemicals we could easily get that would keep you up for three days easy, but you paid a price and his eyes and sallow skin showed the effects already.

"You pulled from her?" I asked. "And is that...?"

I pointed at the screen. He nodded.

"There's a bunch. I went back days. Weeks. Pulled random nights. Some were nothing but this is at least the fourth."

"All fans?"

"All girls. All slaughtered like pigs."

"Damn, dude."

Dru powered down the monitor. I felt like he was going to pitch me on how much money we could make selling these first person murder memories. Didn't even matter she was a celebrity. We had the sensation of plunging a knife into an innocent victim just for the thrill of it captured for anyone else to plug into their brains and experience. Millions. They'd pay millions. But I wanted no part of it.

Then Dru surprised me.

"We gotta stop her."

I sat on that for a second. "How?"

"We gotta take her out, man."

"Let's just call the Forces. They have people to take care of this stuff."

"No cops, man. We stole this shit. I don't even know what the sentence is for something like that."

Probably death. Most everything was death these days. Once euthanasia became federal law for criminals, we'd been killing prisoners like it was a race.

"You think we should kill her?"

"She's gonna keep doing this. She likes it. She loves it. You should see the smile on her face."

I didn't want to. I'd seen it last night.

"But we're not...we don't kill people."

"If we don't do it, it's like we're killing these kids who follow her home. Either way, someone will die."

It didn't happen often, but Dru was right.

FIVE

We drove to her house in the hills, just me and Dru. We had no plan, really, but Dru had a gun. I asked about ballistics and prints and stuff but he wasn't concerned.

"Once they find her murder dungeon, they'll be glad she's dead."

"Where do they dump them?" I asked.

"How the hell should I know?"

"Should we pull more memories and see if we can help the Force figure it out?"

"I told you, man, I don't want them knowing what we did. Those bastards do the same shit that she does, only they wear a uniform and get paid for it."

Fine. Whatever. We'll stop her. A two-man army of justice.

While we were debating, her gate opened and a sleek two-seater slid out near silently into the night. I'd stopped off and filled the hydrogen cell on my shitty hatchback earlier that day so I could follow her for days. That seemed more fun than catching up with her to do what we needed to. Dru prodded my arm and I followed her down the hills and into the crowded streets of Friday night.

Even when I was her age I didn't hit the clubs that hard. We followed her and actor boy through three different dark and humid rooms pulsing with sound, some of it her own music. When a club DJ would see Lindsay Shaw enter the room they would dip into one of her tracks as a nod of respect. I couldn't tell the damn difference between anything anybody played in any of the places we went.

The clubs were loud and dark enough we probably could have done it at any point and nobody would have noticed right away, but neither Dru or I were eager to kill. And Lindy dragged a crowd with her wherever she went like her ass was filled with magnets.

Nearing two in the morning we'd had enough. Dru slid another pill under his tongue and he wouldn't sleep for another twelve hours, but his body protested by aging him ten years in the flickering light show.

"Fuck it," he said. He twisted his torso, feeling the gun at his back, I knew. "Just do it, right?"

"I guess."

He'd been on the verge twice before and nothing had happened. I felt like he was trying to get me to step in and take over, but it was the last thing I wanted to do. Then we saw Lindy and

20

actor boy pluck a wounded gazelle from the herd. An energetic young blonde wearing less than she would on a beach fawned over Lindy. The girl was three, or maybe ten drinks in and her eyes were unfocused. She may have been on any number of other doses of late night fun. Pills, drinks, needles. Who knows? But she walked right into the lion's mouth.

"That girl," Dru said.

"I know."

We shared a look that said now or never. We couldn't let them get this fangirl back to her house. It was weird to be the only one in the room who knew what was going to happen to this innocent fan. Weirder to know that the pop star everyone was genuflecting in front of was about to be dead. But everyone in this club would move on to the next idol to worship within a week, I bet.

Lindy moved toward the bathroom and I tapped Dru.

"Go now. C'mon."

When he didn't move I lifted him and walked with him, skirting around the crowded dance floor and aiming down the dark mouth of the hallway leading to the restrooms. What manner of illicit activity had taken place back here? Probably everything short of murder. Until tonight.

I shoved Dru ahead of me and had serious doubts about his ability to get this done. He'd play acted with the gun, clicking switches, spinning it on his finger, but he looked about to vomit now. Lindy passed into the ladies room and I shoved Dru harder.

"No one's gonna see us or give a shit. Just do it quick and we can get the hell out of here."

The door opened again and a girl came out. I pushed Dru through the opening and the music sounded smothered in cotton once we were inside.

Dru slid the gun out from behind his back and held it tight to his leg. There were five stalls to our right. A long mirror with sinks to our left, one girl applying eye makeup who glanced at us, then turned back to her task without a care.

A flush. The girl seemed satisfied with her eyes and stepped past us. The music flared up like gasoline on a fire as the door opened and shut, then muted again. Lindy Shaw stepped out of a stall. She hesitated. Crazy fans. She was used to it. Guys in the ladies room though, that took it to a new level. Warning bells sounded behind her eyes.

"Not cool, guys. An autograph isn't worth it. You're gonna get kicked the fuck out."

I nudged Dru in his back. He wasn't moving. Dammit, I really didn't want to have to take the gun from him.

She stared us down, hard. "If you want, I can get the Forces involved. Put your asses behind bars. Or do you just want my security to beat you senseless?"

Dru lifted the gun. "You're s..." he choked on the words, had to swallow, then tried again. "You're sick."

Like a coiled spring she leapt. In her hand was a blade I hadn't seen before. She thumbed it open as she moved and Dru had the knife in his thigh before either of us could move. She let out a high pitched martial arts yell, but in that signature voice of hers like she was debuting a new single. Dru let go of the gun and looked down at his leg. She ripped the blade free and quickly stuck him in the belly. She moved like she had a live wire stuck up her ass. Her arm jerked

22

up, dragging the knife north to where it snagged on his sternum. She pulled away and Dru's body opened up.

His guts hit the floor in a splash before he fell forward on top of them.

I tore my eyes away from him to see her looking at me now.

SIX

I'd seen the look in her eyes, the bloodlust. The glee that spilled guts brought out in her. I hadn't wanted to implant that memory out of fear it would be too intense. Here I was living it, making my own memory.

The door opened behind us and two women walked in, laughing. They stopped, looked down at the pile of guts and blood on the floor, screamed and fled. They didn't even notice one of the worlds biggest pop stars right in front of them. Probably wouldn't believe it if they did.

Lindy sprang at me and my flailing attempt to dodge her attack made me slip on the growing pool of Dru's innards. I fell to the floor with him before her slashing knife could reach me. I saw the glinting blade pass over my head as I fell, then my skull cracked off the tile floor. Woozy, I rolled over and put my hand in a wet pile of Dru's intestines. I think that's what they were anyway. I head her high sing-songy voice behind me. I flopped on my back. From under the pile of my friend's guts, my hand had landed on his gun.

Lindy looked me over, her eyes vivisecting me already. She raised the knife, ready to plunge, and I fired.

The gun was tiny. I don't know from calibers or bullets but she slowed, didn't stop. I kept

23

pulling the trigger to little pops no louder than the beat of the music outside in the club. When the gun was empty, Lindy fell to the floor. Her knife tumbled from her hand, bounced off the rim of a toilet in the open stall next to her, and dropped into the water with a splash.

Covered in gore, ready to puke and leaking tears, I ran for the door.

*

I showered at the office in the space we had for workers who pulled all-nighters. The horror of what I'd witnessed played across the inside of my eyelids in a nonstop loop. I could feel it calcifying into something permanent in my brain. A vision I'd never be able to escape.

I fired up the system.

They recommend at least two people for the procedure, but I'd done so many of them I knew I could do it alone. Never done it on myself though.

I needed the memory out of my head. And I needed to get out of town before someone at the club identified me to the Force. Or one of the hundreds of cameras around town spit out my image for everyone to see.

All I would need was one buyer. One sick fucker to set me up in a new life. Trading cash for fantasy. I wonder if they knew what they'd be buying. The gut churning feeling of taking a life.

Setting the probe inside my own brain while trying to check the read-out was difficult but I was determined to get the last two hours extracted from my brain. I pulled the memory, saved it and removed the probe. The next part was gonna suck.

Permanently destroying a memory was still an experimental thing. As far as procedures go it was about as advanced as leeches and amputation with a saw and a shot of whiskey for anesthesia. I had to burn away part of my brain.

Destroy the tissue, destroy the memory.

I'd mapped the spot in my brain so all I had to do was hit the same spot again. Then get the temperature right on the heat probe, hope I didn't miss or get more than I wanted. One half millimeter slip and I'd lobotomize myself.

As I started to calm down and the adrenaline drained from my system, I had a brief moment of hope where I thought I could keep the memory suppressed. Tamp it down until it lay buried under long forgotten childhood traumas and most of the math I ever learned.

Then she came roaring back at me, Blood-soaked and with a war cry as sweet as a songbird. I felt the heat of Dru's innards on my hands, smelled the stink of an open corpse.

I needed it out. Burn it away. Burning away more than I wanted was better than living with this parasite in my skull.

The tip of the probe was warm now. I'd set it in place and it would grow hotter until I could smell my own brain cooking. I watched the monitor, aiming the probe back to where the map said the memory lived. I set it in place, turned up the heat, and waited.

***

©2019 Eric Beetner

Gothic tenements squatted among the steel spikes of skyscrapers crowding the sky. Best part of twenty years Oink had been gone, and even though he was almost a year home, he still marveled at how much Belt City had spread. Not just north and south but upwards. Red lights blinked on rooftops; no other stars were visible. Three tiers of roadway hung over the pedestrian level like scaffolding.

It rained hard in Belt City. Real rain, not the sprinkler stuff he'd gotten used to on Mars. It was freezing, malicious, and wonderful. Some things you didn't even know you'd missed, Oink thought, as he curbed his old biofuel compact and went on foot the rest of the way.

He slid between busy food stalls crammed beneath the up and down ramps, where vendors dished out slices of battered, deep-fried pork belly with noodles, optics of whisky set up behind the steaming cauldrons. There were things even dodgier than the meat under the counters: hash, heroin, coke, and sand—the new product coming out of New Beijing, the smuggling of which cost Oink his job as an NBPD narcotics officer and bought him a return ticket to Earth.

His pension went on a zipper—an exoskeletal spine that kept his back from breaking under the higher gravity of Earth. They did the surgery in transit, while he was in stasis, and he woke to find himself plugged into a wall socket like an old telephone, the zipper grafted onto his back looking like some twitching, grey crustacean, flexing and clicking its pincers as he moved. The doctor explained he had to make sure to keep it charged: green light good, red light bad. To keep himself out of a wheelchair he would need juice, and juice cost money, which he no longer had.

Luckily, he knew some shady people, and shady people were always keen to do you a favor. In just a week he had a new job in private security.

Past the markets, he made his way through a grid of alleys, old-school neon mixing with holos of dancing girls, until he came to a derelict-looking unit with an eyeball cam in its front door. The dead tubes of the antique sign above read: The Solid Air.

The door opened itself into a dingy club for which 'dive bar' must have been the theme it aspired to before it failed. The gang were there already, lounging on burst furniture and drinking from dirty glasses. Good. Oink liked to make them wait.

"Oink, welcome! Make yerself a drink!" Martyn said. The dim lighting of the club made Martyn appear bright and colorful and flat. His projectors and speakers scuttled along in rusting gutters hidden among the A/C and sprinkler pipes above, letting him get up from a tattered Chesterfield and walk over to the bar. Martyn was a ghost, the digitized consciousness of a man dead for over a century. The Solid Air was his place.

"He's late enough as it is," McInnes said. Her long coat was open, the hardware holstered under her arm plain to see. Her eyes were switched off—people were funny about using internal tech around ghosts like Martyn, though he promised he would never dream of hacking his customers—and while temporarily blind, she had this tick of turning her face away from whoever was speaking, giving them her ear instead. "Business. Now," she said, and gave Oink her ear.

Oink flipped out his handheld and cast the image onto the table. "Have a look," he said, because although it was dangerous to wind McInnes up, it was also fun.

The others—Murdough, Sergio, and Braces—crowded round. Braces, so-called because his teeth had been knocked out and replaced with silver dentures that made his mouth look like a bear trap, described the image to his boss, layer by layer.

"The full plans to the mansion," Oink said. "Two more weeks and I'll have the overhaul of the security protocols finished." The floor-by-floor sectional view shifted back into a complete three-dimensional model of Donahue House. Oink swung his hand and the image spun on its axis, a whirl of towers and wings and gables rendered in a blueprint skeleton frame that resolved into a full fleshed image of stone and glass.

*

He pulled up outside the real thing. Took him over an hour to drive from The Solid Air in the west to Donahue House on the outskirts of the east—going pole to pole without taking the maglev was a grind, but his piece-of-crap car wasn't kitted out for it. It was up in the hills and down a long, leafy drive with a grand view of the old town castle.

A strapped and suited guard checked him in at the gate – name was Alexei, Oink knew. He'd insisted on interviews with all current staff when he took on the job of the Donahue's chief of security three months before and fired a few for good measure. He'd passed on a full roster and shift rota to the gang already, including the known schedule of the family: business magnate and current controller of the Donahue fortune, Mr. Parker Donahue; his wife, former globe-trotting socialite and prominent human rights activist,

Mrs. Evelyn Carter-Donahue; and their son, Master Wilhelm Donahue II, heir to the fortune, and, at ten months old, the reason Evelyn Donahue was no longer a socialite or activist.

Oink unplugged his bad back from the port in the car—orange light, fifty-fifty—and climbed the sweeping steps to the front door. It was the ancient face of the building that greeted people at first, the modern additions skulking around the back and sides. Outbuildings testified to all manner of hobbies taken up then abandoned: stables, shooting range, squash court… There was even an observatory where, if he wanted to, Oink could get another look at the New Beijing skyline under its domes—twisting, opalescent spires that looked like dripping tongues of molten glass.

Evelyn met him at the door—she asked him to call her "Evelyn"—wearing pajamas and a robe. Little Will was already in his car seat, bound in blankets, screaming his heart out of his mouth. She swung the seat gently by the handle, *shooshing* softly.

"Thank you so much," she said.

"No problem… Evelyn," Oink said. Their hands brushed for a moment as he took the handle from her. "Come on, wee man, let's hit the road!"

Their ride waited in the basement garage. It belonged to Evelyn—her Sunday run-around piece—an imported two-seater dragster with a hydrogen cell, maglev plates, and surround-view glass, bulletproof, with AR display for enhanced visibility in bad weather and smog. Oink pressed his palm to the door and it opened for him.

It was't long after he started when Evelyn added his biometrics to the security coding on the dragster. He'd been called in late at night, an improper hour. Expecting to speak to Parker Donahue, he was surprised and a little excited to find Evelyn waiting for him instead. She looked rough, hadn't slept more than two hours strung together in ten days, and smelled of stale vomit. Apparently, one of the men he'd fired had been a chauffeur of sorts. One of the few things that could make Master Wilhelm sleep was a ride in the car, and it was this man's job—a secret arrangement between him and Mrs. Donahue—to drive the boy around at night sometimes to give her a rest. "You need to fix this," she said, seething and delirious through deprivation. "Right now." She took him down to the garage and showed him her car. "He likes to go fast," she said.

They went fast. Every few nights, Oink tore down the hillside drive, Will strapped into the passenger seat, tires squealing for grip around the hairpins, and down into the old town where they made for Waverley Station, the east entrance to the maglev motorway—a shining metal viaduct that ran in a straight line through the middle of Belt City, east pole to west pole in the former cities of Edinburgh and Glasgow, respectively.

This night was no different. They hit the motorway and the magnets on the dragster engaged. The computer took over the controls as the car lifted off the road and glided into the empty lane, accelerating to over two hundred miles per hour in five seconds, the G-force crushing Oink into his seat and sending baby Will off to sleep.

The road was quiet, lit only by the headlights of the dragster, whose engine through the toughened glass bubble of the cockpit was softened to a pleasant hum. He could hear the little boy snoring in the seat next to him.

"He's had such a hard start in life," Evelyn said to him one night, weepy-eyed from tiredness and grateful to hand the boy over. She didn't elaborate and Oink didn't ask. Born the first son of a billionaire mogul, *lucky little punk*, what's hard about that?

Two realizations irked him in the quiet—the fact he enjoyed this time driving the boy about in the speedy car, and the fact he also did it to please Evelyn.

In ten minutes, the maglev ended and he took control again, saving him from his thoughts. He cruised the business district where the roads were smoother then headed down for a pit stop— he fancied a haggis bowl (*the things you miss!*).

An old banger, worse than his own compact, cut him up and he slammed the brakes and the horn. When they came to the next set of lights the driver got out. Something flashed in the driver's hand—a tire iron maybe. Oink reached inside his jacket and unbuttoned the holster that held his modded police-issue crowd-suppressor. He slid his fingers into the grip of his shock knuckles and lowered the window, smiling.

"Nice car, pal, say—" the driver cut off mid-sentence and broke into a smile that showed sharpened, silver teeth. "Oink! What the hell are ye doin' round here in *that* thing? I was ready to jack ye!"

"I was hopin' ye'd try!" Oink laughed and held up his hand to show the Volt-Punch.

"Does this thing belong to the Donahues?" Braces tried to whistle but it didn't work because of his teeth. He ducked his head to get a look into

32

the interior. "Who's yer buddy there? Is that the Donahue bairn?"

Oink nodded. Their eyes met in a loaded stare. "Cute kid," Braces said, breaking off with a smile. He made his excuses and left.

Oink forgot all about his Haggis bowl and blasted off back to the maglev, launching them away from the west pole and back towards the house he was supposed to help McInnes, Braces and the gang rob in a couple of weeks.

*

He didn't sleep well during the day, then as the sun went down he got the call he'd been worrying about getting. McInnes's flat voice: "The Solid Air, two hours."

He didn't want to leave it to chance to be the last one in this time, so he arrived early and staked out a place where he watched them arrive. He checked his gear—the gun was hacked to allow full-automatic fire and if he sprayed the room he could punch a hole in each of them and reduce the walls to studs and timbers in seconds, if it came to that.

He'd made sure the zipper was fully charged and switched on the heavy-lifting power boost. They were all handy in a fist fight—Braces was the weak link physically—and even blind, he wouldn't count McInnes out. She was a veteran of the North American Wars where she lost her eyes, eaten away by nanobots from a spore bomb. Rumor was it wasn't just her eyes they had to replace—she'd spent a year undergoing a battery of therapeutic treatments for her mind: shock therapy, hallucinogenic therapy, VR therapy… War turned her into an animal so science created a human suit for her to wear.

Then there was Martyn, who could kill the lights or bombard him with folk music on the club's speakers. Joking aside, Oink knew little about Martyn. The ghost was obviously connected, but he wasn't McInnes's boss, nor did he work for her. He apparently provided the club—his home and prison—out of generosity and loneliness.

Oink stomped in, brusque from the off. "What's this about? I'm busy, ye know. And every meetin' adds to the likelihood of givin' ourselves away."

McInnes's ear twitched towards him. Blind, using her ears and nose to track, the animal seemed closer to the surface. "Braces said ye were out drivin' the Donahue boy last night."

"He has a big mouth," Oink said. "Literally."

Braces smirked, *who me?*

"Got us thinkin' maybe there's another angle to this thing," McInnes said.

"I hand over the lad, ye ransom him for the sum of the Donahue fortune, daddy pays over the cash to see his little boy again. Easy money, right?"

"Right."

"Wrong. Sure, ye're thinkin', but not thinkin' hard. First, the only son of a multi-billionaire livin' in Belt City is obviously gonnae be lo-jacked. Wean's got tracers pingin' out his ears."

"We could sort that."

"Second, he's ten months old, how are ye gonnae feed him? Who's changin' him when he craps himself? Where's he gonnae sleep?"

He could see Braces grinning.

"Third—and I can't believe I have to say this— *I'm not a fuckin' child snatcher!*"

34

"Aw, he's sweet on the bairn," Braces said, chuckling and trying to get everyone to join in. "Or maybe he's sweet on mummy, is that it?"

Oink plastered a big grin onto his face and everyone stopped laughing, except Braces, who often failed to read a room. *Good.* He slammed his fist straight into the gurning moron's nose, yielding a satisfying crunch and twin jets of blood. Braces fell back but Oink caught him by the collar, pulled him in again and planted two more, blood choking the man as it ran into his throat.

Nobody moved to intervene, yet. Sergio and Murdough, both resplendent in their oil-stain camo shell suits—they obscured you on security feeds and had become a uniform for gangsters and posers—waited for an order. McInnes hadn't moved from her seat, though Oink could see her straining to listen. He imagined she could smell the blood.

He pulled out the Volt-Punch, buzzing and bristling to be let loose, and held it to Braces's mouth. "How d'ye reckon this would feel going through those teeth, huh?"

Now McInnes spoke: "Enough, Oink. It was just a suggestion."

"Just a suggestion? Do ye really understand what ye're suggesting? This boy is the heir to the Donahue fortune. Ye know the term 'hot property'? Even if ye got the money there's no way ye could just give him back and disappear. Ye'd have to kill him. Which one of ye is gonnae pull the trigger on a baby? Braces? Or one of these two clowns?" He turned on the muscle-heads, who looked down at their feet. Then he faced McInnes. This would be a direct challenge. If it went bad it would be quickest draw wins. "No,

I think it would be left up to the boss here. Are ye baby killer, McInnes?"

The air in the room was heavy. Martyn flickered on the side-lines, the exasperated bartender in a western, expecting his business is about to get trashed for the nth time.

"Calm down, Oink," she said.

He eased up. "I've been workin' this plan for months. It's meticulous. In two weeks, I'll have access to everythin', ye can take the family jewels from the god damn safe if ye want it. And most important, we get out clean, no mess."

"Sure. Sure."

He let them leave first, Braces being carried by Sergio, Murdough guiding McInnes out the door where she could switch her eyesight back on. Oink couldn't do the same with his zipper, unless he wanted to roll in on a chair. He wasn't sure if this ingratiated him to Martyn in some way or made him vulnerable.

"It's some high-wire act ye've got there," the ghost said.

"Can I have a whisky?"

"Help yerself." Martyn led the way, projectors and speakers rattling along above. "There's nothin' wrong with wantin' to keep the bairn safe," he added.

"Actually, hold that whisky, I better be off."

*

Two weeks later, everything was set. It was the night before the robbery and Oink was taking Will out for a spin. The family were jetting off in the morning and Evelyn would need a good sleep—it was Oink who'd suggested he take the boy that night. He tried not to think too much about that, or the smile Evelyn had given him, as he sped off down the winding hill.

36

The car launched down the bullet track of the floating motorway on autopilot. Oink hadn't yet found the station he liked when the proximity warning of the rear parking sensor flashed up red. A video feed of a van appeared—nearly bumper to bumper. It whizzed round and up the side of the car, scraping paint and sending the alarm into a frenzy. The noise woke Will, who joined in the riot with his howls.

The van pulled in sharp in front—the thing must have been hacked for manual steering—causing the dragster to slow down. Oink thumped at the useless steering wheel. Hovering just ahead, the back doors of the van opened and a figure wearing a motorcycle helmet and a shell suit lunged out—a bungee cord whipped out behind him, harnessing him to the van—and landed on the dragster's front end, making it dip and correct. He popped the top off a spike grenade and planted it right where Oink could see it from within, his gun pointing but not firing, impotent within the bullet-proof bubble of the dragster's cockpit.

A light on top of the spike started to flash and the bomber leapt off—the dragster continuing to slow, the van pulling away ahead.

Oink ripped at the door handles—sealed. The grenade flashed. He punched at the windows and bloodied his knuckles. Three, two, one—

The flashing light died and so did the dragster's headlights and AR display. Pain shot through Oink's back, skull to tail, and the car dropped and hit the surface of the road, doubling down on the jarring agony, like his back had been split in two.

As soon as the car touched down, crash spray hosed from the roadside sprinklers, bringing the

37

skidding car to a stop as the foam hardened around it.

Will screamed. Oink screamed. He couldn't move, he was pinned. His arms and legs wouldn't budge and he couldn't see anything through the foam shell that glued the car in place.

Slowly, the foam over the passenger side started to melt. From the corner of his eye—he couldn't turn his head—he saw the crash foam get eaten away. Someone was spraying it with acid. Soon it was eating through the paintwork. An exploding lockpick punched a hole through the door and it swung open, letting in the acrid stench of the acid, the melting foam, and the burnt paint.

A head popped in, the face obscured by a nose-splint, the eyes on either side being swallowed by purple-black bruises, the lips opening to reveal a metal-toothed smile.

Will screamed as his straps were cut and he was lifted from his seat.

"Kids, such a handful, eh?" Braces said.

Oink could do nothing. His gun lay dead in his lifeless hand.

*

The police had him pointlessly handcuffed to a gurney in a private hospital room, where he lay on his belly, immobile. No slack for an ex-cop. He told them exactly what had happened on the road but left out all the rest. They asked a lot of questions and were very interested in his exile from Mars.

They'd recovered the bomb from the car—an EMP, which had taken out not just the car's systems but fried Oink's zipper as well. A tech could get him up and running in no time but the

38

doctors wanted to scan his back first to make sure everything was still where it should be.

Mr. and Mrs. Donahue were there too—it was back to "Mrs. Donahue" now. She explained her arrangement with Oink to the detective, Parker's look of fury unable to settle on either one for the moment, as if he'd found out they were having an affair. She handed over her computer, palmed the lock, and fired up the tracking program but it showed nothing.

"EMP will have cooked any electronic devices on or within the child," the detective said. He made a show of sounding sorry about all this but Oink could tell he was enjoying these rich people floundering in distress. Oink would have too, if it wasn't Will and it wasn't Evelyn and it wasn't all his fault.

"No! Oh God, oh Jesus, no…" Evelyn nearly fell down. She grabbed Parker by the arm. His face had lost its color, like all his blood had drained into his shoes.

"Sorry, 'cooked' is just an expression, no harm will have come to him physically, see, an *el-ec-tro-mag-ne-tic pulse* is a—"

"I know what it is! It's his heart. Will's heart…"

Oink felt something cold leak through him, spilling down the bones and metal of his spine under the thrum of numbing agents and painkillers. *He had such a hard start in life…*

"…He has a regulator…" She was crying now, and between words she sobbed into the collar of her husband's shirt. The man just stood there stiff. "Will was born too early… he was so *small*, and he… had problems with his heart and lungs and other things too… all the surgery, God, we practically lived in the hospital… they fitted him up with all sorts of gadgets to keep things

39

going…" Evelyn started to sob, a pitiful whimper that reanimated her husband. He pulled up a chair for her. "I'll get you some water," he said, and took the detective outside to have someone to yell at.

As the soon as the door closed, Evelyn stopped crying and fixed Oink with a Baltic glare. "You know where he is," she said. "Why aren't you telling us?"

"The polis will only make things worse. I can sort this."

"You'd better. If his regulator isn't working, his heart could fail at any moment."

"Then get me out of here. Bribe the cops and bribe the docs, give them whatever it takes to get me walkin'. I'll bring Will back and ye'll never have to see me again. I promise."

"You bring Will back to me—*alive*—then I'll decide whether I turn you in or not."

"Agreed."

*

Oink parked by the alley and waded through decades of abandoned furniture and rotting appliances to reach the back door of The Solid Air. There was no camera here and the door looked much less heavy duty. Still, he turned the boost up on the zipper and every kick jarred something not quite right in his spine.

The door buckled in a screech of sheared metalwork and Oink stepped inside to meet the barrel of a nasty-looking gun and a pair of swollen eyes behind the sights.

"Shit, I thought it might be the polis," Braces said.

Oink held his hands up. "I'm not here to make trouble, I just need to see if the boy is okay."

"Shit." He was chewing his lips with his silver teeth. "Everythin's gone fuckin' sideways," he said. "Somethin's wrong with the kid. He seemed awright till we got back, then…"

Oink could hear raised voices coming from the lounge. "Let me help." He moved in close, hands still up.

Braces lowered the gun to his side. Oink swung a penalty kick at the goon's crotch. Braces shrieked and choked as if his balls were coming up through his throat. He dropped to his knees; the gun clattered to the floor.

"That was for leavin' me in that car," Oink said. He slid the shock knuckles onto his fist and made sure they were turned up full, fizzing. "And this is just cause I want to." He slammed the Volt-Punch into the man's metal teeth.

The screams followed him through the maze of back corridors that twisted through cloakrooms and liquor cages.

As he approached the main room, he could make out Martyn shouting something like, "He's gonnae die otherwise!" Then McInnes quite clearly answered, "Better for him if he does."

Oink strode in, gun raised—safety off, full-auto on. "Where's the kid? Hand him over. Now." He had the drop on them, they knew it.

McInnes turned her ear to him, probably smelled gun oil. "On the table," she said, pointing in slightly the wrong direction.

Will was lying on the scratched and sticky coffee table within the nook of chairs where they held their meetings. He was still and pale and, for the first time to Oink, seemed terribly small and frail. "Is… Is he dead?" They looked at each other. "IS HE DEAD!?" He let each of them feel the stare of gun's eye, the two lunks flinching away, McInnes standing her ground. He wondered if she felt the laser sight on her skin.

"Not yet, but he will be if we don't do somethin' soon." Martyn stood between Oink and the gang. "We need to get that regulator workin' again. It needs power. If we connect up to it... Yerself and McInnes both have—"

"I already said, 'no way', *ghost*," McInnes said. "Oink—" Whatever she was about to say to him was cut off by the muffled scream of Braces, who burst into the room. Oink had just a second to clock the blood running from the man's eyes, ears, and nose, and the stands of oozing, melting silver on his lips, congealing strands of it gluing up his tongue, before the shooting started.

Braces opened up on them, scattering them among the furniture that burst into firewood and feathers. Murdough was hit in the volley, one ear gone and a hole in his throat. Oink rolled on the deck and came up shooting. The crowd-suppressor turned Braces into a cheese grater, then he caught one in the shoulder as Sergio turned on him from behind the bar. Oink took up a position behind a pillar and returned fire, but McInnes forced him to move—she was shooting something large caliber, blind, from behind a chair. Shots going wide but getting closer. He dodged out, lending covering fire to himself by spraying bullets in a wide arc across the bar, glass and booze raining down on Sergio who squealed, "Stop! Stop!" McInnes zeroed in on the voice and blasted her canon into the bar.

Sergio taken care of, it was just Oink and McInnes left, creeping in the fog of gun smoke and plasterwork snow. He needed a line of sight that didn't come so close to the baby unconscious on the table. He picked up a whisky bottle that had escaped intact and lobbed it across the room. Hearing the smash, McInnes darted out, and so did Oink. He pulled the trigger and the gun clicked empty.

She faced him across the room, canon pointed in his direction. He stood still, held his breath. Her ears strained to catch him, head tilting this way and that, reaching out with all her other senses. Then she sighed, lifted a hand up behind her ear, and flipped the switch. There was a flicker as her eyes came on, the irises flushed with color and twisted as they focused. "Last shot," she said, walking towards him, gun trained right at his head now. "Had to be sure it was a hit. We could still walk away, ye know."

"And let the boy die?"

"There are things worse than death, Oink. I know."

"I can save him."

"It's too late." She took aim. "Bye." She gave a slight smile then her mouth went slack, as if the power to her body had been cut. Her eyes were no longer focusing on the target but looking somewhere beyond. "What… what… fuck, oh on, oh no…" She spun this way and that. Her hands flew up to her face. "Get away! Get away!" She shrieked and ran from Oink, throwing herself up against the pillars and furniture and flailing on the floor, clawing at herself. She disappeared into the back rooms, braying like some wild, wounded thing, itching as if infested.

The boy was cold. Oink put his ear the baby's bare chest and listened.

"It's too late to call ambulance." Projectors whirred and Martyn rematerialized. "We need to go in now."

"How?"

"Yer charger cable. He needs to borrow yer battery. With a little juice in him I can go in and see what's goin' on."

"'Go in' as in 'hack in'?"

"Oink, he's been in arrest for over a minute, we don't have time to talk. McInnes should've done it already but then everythin' kicked off…"

Oink looked for the port—it was behind the ear, difficult to see because of the quality of the graft, the entire cable reel internal. He connected his own cable to it. "Now what?"

It hit him. Light flashed behind his eyes, he flushed hot and cold, his back prickled and burned, as if the zipper boost had been pushed over its limit. He was on fire, he felt like he could pull the whole building down to the foundations. He saw stars, a universe, spinning out in his head. Something thumped, thumped, thumped, getting closer and louder until it was the only thing he could hear and it filled him up and he couldn't breathe with it.

The lights flickered and burst. Oink felt the energy drain out of him in a rush that left him giddy and confused, lying on the floor in the dark. When the need to puke passed, he fumbled around for Will. He grabbed hold of his charger cable and followed the length of it.

The boy was there, eyes still closed. Oink put his head to the baby's chest again and held his breath. *Thump-thump-thump*, a rapid, shallow pulse. A sigh shivered out of the boy's mouth. Relief made Oink giddy again. He wrapped Will in his long coat and headed for the front door— locked electronically and too sturdy for Oink to kick down. His zipper light was in the red now and working for two. "Martyn? Martyn, get the damn door open!" But there was no answer. The club was silent.

He fumbled his way through the back rooms and out into the alley. McInnes was sitting on the ground, back against a rusted old chest freezer. Her face and hands were covered in blood. Her eyelids were sunken inwards into the recesses where her eyes used to be. Her breathing was ragged. "Oink?" she said.

"I've got the wean, McInnes, move an inch and I'll cut ye in half."

"This wasn't what I wanted. The call came from higher up."

"You ran it up the flag pole after all?"

She shook her head, sending blood running down her cheeks like tears. Oink noticed a bloody eyeball in her lap, the fiber cables trailing out the back like a tail. "No. Not us. I agreed with what you said… Must've been someone else."

"Who?"

"That bastard got me a good one. Motherfucker. Knew about the boy's heart too…"

Oink's charge light was blinking, he needed to get Will home. He headed for the car, the little body pressed against his chest starting to heat up. On his way, he felt something crunch and burst under his foot.

*

Evelyn was waiting up, ran out as soon as she saw Oink pull up outside.

He handed the baby over and detached the cable. "Get him plugged in right now. I could take him to the hospital…" She turned away to the house without a word for him—he deserved that much, at least it looked like she hadn't called the cops.

Evelyn hefted Will up onto her shoulder. He'd woken up and was looking at Oink. Oink thought he might miss those late-night rides with the little guy—you never know what you'll miss. He waved and Will stared right back with eyes that were a hundred years old.

***

©2019 Callum McSorley

BAD SCORE

REBEL PREACHERS

NEW GATE CITY

It's not every day you go to sleep as a brunette and wake up as a blonde—but that was what happened to me. I woke in a seedy motel with a single, fly-stained window, looking out on a graffiti-sprayed overpass, under a golden brown sky the texture of burnt toast. My new body was in a cheap red backless dress like a hooker would wear for a prom date.

I had no memory of how I'd got here—but someone else was in the room, standing in the darkest corner near the window. The stranger was smoking a joint, looking out at the street. He was tall and wide-shouldered. I couldn't see details of him in the darkness because the bright sunlight hurt my eyes, but I did see a gun tucked in the back of his jeans.

Slowly, I sat up and looked down at my new body, seeing big breasts, a flat stomach, long legs and creamy white skin. I groaned. I looked like every clichéd fantasy girl from a prepubescent boy's mind, but I didn't like it. I used to be mixed race with a gym-hard body and a life's worth of beautiful tattoos on my skin, reminding me of all the good times and bad ones. Now I was a blank-slate, a cybernetic brain inside a synthetic body.

How did I end up here? Had the stranger done things to me? I wanted to grab his gun, but the barest movement was making the mattress squeak. There was no way to cross the room without him hearing me, even if he was stoned. That gun was a huge problem.

My new eyes adjusted dilation until I could see the man better. He was dressed like a cowboy in jeans, alligator boots, rhinestone jacket and a plaid shirt. His face was scarred from his right brow to his square jaw. He was handsome but his skin was weather-beaten like old leather. His name alluded me for a couple of seconds, but then it snapped into my mind with a rush of confusing emotions. I loved and hated this man. He was my husband.

"Brandon?" I said. "What the hell happened to me?"

He sighed and sucked on his joint before turning and answering. "Someone murdered you, Maggie."

The cold truth hit me hard. Of course—that was why I was in another body. "When? Why? Where?"

"I don't know the why," Brandon said, "but it was six months ago just outside New Gate City—on the American side. A state trooper found you dumped in the desert with your brain pulped and your cyber implants fried. Since then, your mind's been digitally stored in the stacks until I could rent you a new body. I hope you like what I got, Maggie. You always wondered what it would be like to be blonde and white, like the popular girls in your high school."

"Yeah—I envied those bitches, but I didn't really want to be one. I can't believe this. You uploaded me into a blonde sex doll? You couldn't get me something that looked a bit more like the original me, Bran?"

He looked hurt. "Hey—I didn't get much choice, baby. You died and left me *alone*. Besides, this ain't Mexico, where you can choose your own doll before you die. We don't have universal healthcare. You get what you pay for in the Bad Old USA."

"I know that!" I snapped. "But this is the best you could do?"

"Maggie, I sold *everything* so I could bring you back. Look!" He showed me his bare hand, with a white line where the skin wasn't tanned. "I had to pawn my wedding ring. Don't get mad at me. I thought you'd be *pleased to wake up alive again.* Beats the alternative, right?"

"I am pleased, believe me—but it's a shock, Bran. Hell, I am grateful for everything. I love you for doing this. But I have so many questions. My head's spinning. God! This is so weird!"

I paced around the tiny bedroom, feeling strange because I was a different height and weight. It felt like I was wearing someone else's shoes. I kept tripping over my feet and banging into the furniture. Brandon stubbed out his joint and moved quickly to stop me falling over and breaking something. "Hey! Be careful, babe. It's a rental. Any damage comes out of the deposit."

"Oh, God, things just get worse and worse. Look at me! I can't even walk like an adult!"

"You'll get used to it," he promised.

"This isn't me!" I said. Tears ran down my cheeks. "The real me is dead."

"Your mind's the same," he said. "That's what counts. Not the flesh and bones."

He held me and I wept.

"I missed you every second," he said, holding me, hugging me. He was still taller than me, but only by a few inches. I sobbed into his shoulder, then pulled away, hating myself for crying. It was weak. Maggie Ortez wasn't weak. She was a tough bitch.

"I can't believe I was *murdered*. Last thing I remember, I was going to sleep in comfy hotel in Paradise Springs. Did I get killed in my sleep?"

"No," he said. "You called me the next morning—after your mind had been backed up during your REM sleep."

All humans fitted with cyber implants had their new memories transferred from their organic brain to a safe, encrypted storage site when they were sleeping. Their backup personas were store forever in a digital format, providing a form of immortality for anyone rich enough to afford a new physical body. "So, I lost only one day of memories?"

Brandon nodded. "Remember I was up north doing a deal? You called me and told me you were going to see Tommy Cruz about a big score in New Gate City. I heard nothing after that until a cop called me, telling me your corpse had been found. The cops didn't know about the score, of course. I kept that secret. I wanted to find Cruz and personally get the truth out of him by any method. I looked for him everywhere, but nobody's seen him. It's like he disappeared off the face of the planet. The man's vanished like a politician's promises."

"Tommy could be dead," I said. "Maybe he was dumped somewhere else, where he hasn't been found yet?"

"Yeah, I did wonder. I checked online activity on his stacked persona. There's been no updates after you went missing, which means he's dead or he turned off his updates to go dark. Did anyone else know about the score, Maggie?"

"Not from me," I said. "Tommy could've talked, though. Or he could have double-crossed me, but I have a hard time believing either. We served together during the Downfall. He was in my unit and I trusted him with my life."

"Times change," Brandon said. "Cruz could've betrayed you. Can you remember *why* you were meeting him?"

"No. He was very excited, though. Told me the score was worth millions. Something clearly went wrong. I was so stupid. I should never had done a job without you watching my back, Bran. I'm sorry. I screwed up. Hell—I need a toke on that joint, pronto."

"It won't affect you," Brandon said. "That model doesn't have narcotic processing."

"Son of a bitch!"

"I've got more bad news, Maggie."

"What's worse than dying and not being able to get high?"

"You know I told you the doll is just a rental?"

"Yeah?"

"I could only afford 48 hours."

"And then what happens?"

"You'll go back into the stacks."

"I don't believe this. I've got two days of life?"

"47 hours now," he said.

"Bran, this doesn't make a whole lot of sense. Why'd you bring me back *now*? What was so urgent?"

My husband looked down at his feet, avoiding eye contact. "Maggie, I need your help."

"What did you do?" I said.

"Nothing! I swear! A couple of days ago, I was in a bar in Reno when two bikers tried to kidnap me in the parking lot. I got away—but they shot me. Clipped me in the arm." Brandon pulled back his sleeve to show me a dirty, blood-stained bandage. "I'm okay—but they're after me and I don't have a clue why. I ain't got no enemies. I figured it had to do with your big score. That's why I had to bring you back. I was hoping you could at least work out why someone wanted to grab me, then I could figure out what to do about it."

"The bikers. You see their patches?"

"Yeah. They were Rebel Preachers."

The gang had thousands of members. They were the biggest MC on the West Coast of New America. They ran dope and human trafficking on the border, sneaking people and drugs into Mexico. "Their MC is based in New Gate City. It's got to be connected to the big score. I guess me and Tommy Cruz stole a lot of money from them. They must have worked out I was involved – so they came after you looking for their money, thinking I must have told you something."

"Makes sense," Brandon said. "But where's their money?"

"I don't have a clue," I said. "Obviously, the Rebel Preachers don't have it—so that's some good news. It means the money's out there—somewhere."

"That is good news." Brandon grinned. "With that money, you could buy a better doll from Mexico and we could have a new life."

"If we can find it before they find us," I said. "I might be able learn what happened to the money if I can find Tommy. Luckily, I know where Maria, his abuelita, lives. She'll talk to me—but I can't show up at her home dressed like a hooker. Got enough money to buy me a better outfit?"

"Barely," he said. "I saw a thrift store down the street sells clothes. I'll go and get you something."

"No," I said. "I don't trust your taste, Bran. You'd come back with a tube top and a mini skirt. I'll choose my own clothes."

He gave me some five hundred bucks—enough to buy some cheap clothes with no change. With a whole biker gang looking for us, I didn't want to go outside unarmed.

"Bran, you got a gun for me?"

"Sorry," he said. "I didn't have time to get another piece. I've been on the run."

"Where exactly are we?"

"Geektown."

That was a low-rent area of New Gate City. Close to the heart of the Rebel Preachers' territory. "Why'd you bring me here?"

"I figured it was last place they'd look."

Smart and dumb. Typical Brandon. "Have you got wheels?"

"Yeah. A stolen pickup. Parked a block away."

"You get the car," I said. "I'll go shopping. Pick me up on the corner in ten."

The store was filled with racks of old clothes at discount prices. I grabbed anything in my new size. I was soon feeling a little more like myself, wearing a dark leather jacket, black jeans and kick-ass red boots. I added a dark baseball cap to tuck my blonde hair under. The sun beat down on me like a cop's baton while I waited for Brandon. A black pickup stopped next to me. A face leered out—white and bearded.

"Hey, girl, how much for a good time?"

"More than you can afford," I said.

The driver called me a whore and drove away.

I looked around for Brandon. The revving of a motorbike engine sent my new heart into overdrive. A group of a dozen bikers stopped at the light, checking me out like a piece of meat. They wore Rebel Preacher patches on their leather jackets—skeletons holding burning

Bibles. I felt like running, but I had nowhere to go. The light changed and they drove off—in the direction of the motel, where they stopped. They parked their bikes and spread out, blocking the exits. I could see them heading for our room. My heart beat quicker. Somehow they'd traced us. If we'd not left ten minutes ago, we would have been trapped. Where was Brandon?

Another pickup slowed down. A rust bucket belching fumes. Brandon was driving it, hiding his face under a baseball cap. I jumped in the passenger side.

"Go!" I ordered. "They've found the motel."

Brandon cursed. "They must've told the manager to look out for me. These scars make me kind of recognisable."

We couldn't hurry, but we wasted no time leaving the area. I kept looking back expecting to see the bikers chasing us, but the road was clear. Brandon rubbed sweat off his forehead. "So, what's Tommy's grandmother's address?"

I told him where Maria lived. It would take four hours to get there—so I spent the time learning more about my doll's functions.

The doll didn't come with a printed instruction manual, but I quickly worked out how to access the cyber-brain's retinal display. I simply had to think commands to make the internal menus visible. The date of manufacture was 2041. Information appeared inside my head, overlaying in my vision field. I displayed the current time allowed in my rental body before I was shut out:

56

46 hours and 18 minutes. It was useful info so I left the time ticking down while linking into the local wi-fi network, calling up news feeds, helping me get up to date on the state of the world.

Not much had changed in six months. America was still a mess after the Downfall. We had a new president as bad as the old one. Mexico was still our wealthy neighbour, trying to keeping illegal immigrants out. Canada was still fighting the Anarchy Rebellion. It was all depressingly familiar. Eventually, I could stand it no longer and switched off my feed. I rode the rest of the way in silence.

Tommy's abuelita lived in a small Latino community outside the city. The houses were small and prefabricated from the cheapest materials—but they were good compared with the ones I'd lived in as a kid, growing up in Los Angeles during the Rioting Twenties. They all had neat lawns and no bullet holes in the walls. Maria's was a pretty pink one with a neat rose garden and a pink picket fence. We parked outside, next to a small red solar car.

"Stay here," I told Brandon. "She'll be freaked out when I show up in a different body. She's a frail woman in her eighties. You'll only scare her into a heart attack."

"But I should stay with you."

"Just guard the outside, Cowboy."

The air smelled of freshly cut grass. I breathed in the sweet scent as I walked to the screen door and knocked lightly. A young Latina woman opened the door. She was barefooted and wearing a yellow summer dress. She was very beautiful.

"Yes?" she said. "How can I help you?"

"I'm looking for Maria Cruz."

"Who can I say is asking for her?" she said, suspiciously.

"Maggie Ortez."

"Come in," she said. "She's sleeping – but I'll take you to her."

I stepped inside and she closed the door behind me – then felt the cold barrel of a gun poking into my back. I froze. "Hey – what's going on?"

"You're not Maggie Cruz," she said. "She's dead."

"Yes, I died," I said. "But I'm alive again. I'm in this doll."

"Liar. Prove you're really her or I'll blow you apart."

"Prove how?"

"Tell me what Maggie accidentally broke on her last visit."

"Uh—there's was a little porcelain statue of the Virgin Mary on a dresser. I caught it on the sleeve of my coat. It smashed into pieces. The head rolled off down the hall like a marble. I was so embarrassed, but Maria saw it and laughed."

The gun was removed. "It really is you!"

I faced the young woman, frowning. "I know who I am—but who are you?"

"It's me! Maria! I'm also in a new doll. I was dying of cancer when I last saw you. I got this lovely replacement body thanks to my Tommy. He paid for it so I could be young again. He's a good grandson."

Maria's doll was an excellent model, far superior to mine. I felt a spark of jealousy. "It must have cost a fortune."

"I didn't ask where he got the money," she said. "It just arrived one day in a package about four months back. Enough to pay for my second life. The original me passed away a few weeks later. Coming back in this body was a miracle. I'm twenty again! It's a dream come true!"

"That's fantastic," I said. "Maria, I'm looking for Tommy. I desperately need his help. Do you know where I can find him?"

"You're not the first person to ask me that," she said. "A few days after you died, two men dressed like cops came around, asking me if I had seen my grandson. They said Tommy was a witness to a serious crime so they needed to find him, to protect him. They acted like they wanted to help Tommy. I didn't believe a word they said. I wasn't born yesterday. They weren't cops. One had a tattoo on his wrist—a snake twisted around a skull. No cop would wear that. The other looked like the Hulk – muscles on his muscles. Straight away, I knew my Tommy was in trouble because I hadn't seen or talked to him in a week. He normally visits me at the weekend or at least calls or sends an email. But he hadn't contacted me. I knew he was in trouble. I told them I didn't know where Tommy was. It was the truth—so they believed me, fortunately. The so-called cops asked me to call them when Tommy showed up. I lied and promised them I would. Idiots. I'd never give up blood to a couple of fake cops. They wanted to do something bad to him, don't they?"

"Yeah," I said. "They're Rebel Preachers—the biker gang. It looks like Tommy stole some money from them and somehow they found out."

Maria crossed herself. "Did they kill you because you were working with Tommy?"

"I think so," I said. "Can you help me find Tommy, abuelita?"

"Mija, I'd tell you if I knew. He's probably in Mexico, living the high life. That's what I dream. He's wise to stay away. He's safe wherever he is."

"I need Tommy's help. Is there a way for you to contact him?"

"Tommy always said that if I needed to contact him in an absolute emergency to leave a coded message with one of his old army buddies. Tommy called him the Russian. Do you know who that is?"

"Yeah," I said. "There was a guy in our unit called Ivan. The Russian was his nickname, even though he was from the Ukraine and hated it. I haven't seen him in years. He's a recluse, living up in Alaska somewhere."

"I'm supposed to call The Russian and leave my coded message. Then Tommy will contact me."

"Can you call Ivan right now? I've only got a day and a half in this body before I go back to the stacks permanently—unless I can pay for a new body. To me, that counts as an emergency."

"For you, mija? I'll do it. Tommy left me a burner phone. Excuse me, mija. I'll make the call for you. Oh - you might as well invite the man in the car inside for a cold beer. Is he your husband?"

"Yeah – that's Brandon."

I invited my husband inside. Brandon and I waited in the kitchen, watching the young Maria making a call in the back yard. I explained what had happened to her. Brandon's ogled Maria's slim figure. "That hottie is Tommy's grandmother? Damn. I wish I could have got that body for you."

"Admiring another woman in front of me ain't cool, Bran."

"Yeah – but look at her. She's smoking. Any guy would chew his own arm off for a shot at her."

I punched him on the arm and he winced like it really hurt. "Jeez! What you do that for, babe? That's where I was shot."

I'd forgotten that. "Sorry. But you deserved it. You know I got a jealous streak. Uh—looks like your bleeding. Take off your jacket and shirt so I can take a look."

"It's not important."

"Do it, Bran."

Reluctantly, Brandon stripped down to his waist to let me examine his bandage. Blood was seeping through. It needed changing. By then Maria had finished making her call. She came back and saw the wet bandage. "That's filthy and needs changing. I'll get some things from the bathroom."

When Maria returned with a medical kit, I moved Brandon's rhinestone jacket off the table so she could put it down next to Brandon. Some loose change and other things fell out of a pocket, like some chewing gum packets. I picked them up and put them back while Maria cleaned Brandon's wound. Brandon groaned. Maria asked me for something, but I was distracted by thoughts. If Tommy had not betrayed me, that meant someone else had. There were not many suspects. Brandon had known about the big score – but I couldn't believe he would kill me for money. We'd been married for ten years. He had loved my original body too much to harm me. I would have split the cash with him—so that left a third party, currently unknown. Maria spoke again.

"Sorry," I said. "What did you say?"

"Can you get me the anti-septic spray?"

"Uh—sure."

Maria did an expert job of cleaning Brandon's wound. Afterwards, there was nothing we could do until Tommy contacted Maria via the burner phone, which she left on the kitchen table. Maria made some tortillas. Brandon laid down on a couch and dozed. I watched some more news feeds in the living room. I didn't need sleep in my new doll because my brain was entirely inorganic, requiring no rest.

I had a long time to think while I waited. I learnt more about the doll I was inhabiting. It was a fairly basic model based on the biomechanical advances in military robots prior to the Downfall. It had a battery at its core meant to last a year before recharging. It also had a limit set to the energy output that made its reflexes no faster than an ordinary human's. I searched the net for ways to hack my own body, which was illegal, but that wasn't going to stop me. I found a way to change the output parameters, shortening the battery life to a few days, increasing strength and speed. It would damage the doll's cybernetic systems, but I didn't care about that. I needed to make my body into a weapon. I hacked my own control systems, suddenly feeling a rush of acceleration to my limbs, overclocking my cyber brain. A mosquito flying past started to slow down in flight so I could see its wings flapping. I stood in a micro-second and crossed the room in a heartbeat. I caught the mosquito in my hand before it had a chance to move – then released it outside in the same second. Everything around me was almost static. I moved my fingers so fast they blurred. Warning symbols flashed in my head. CORE TEMPERATURE RISING TO DANGEROUS LEVEL. I could smell burning. My skin was started to peel off. Okay – that was enough of a test. I reduced my speed quickly back to the normal parameters, then raced to the bathroom to strip off my clothes and cool down in an ice-cold shower. CORE TEMPERATURE NORMAL. I stepped out shivering. I was getting redressed when the burner phone rang.

I hurried into the kitchen to see Brandon watching Maria speaking on the phone. Maria was nodding. "Yes—she's here now. Maggie—it's Tommy."

She handed me the phone.

"Maggie?" a muffled voice said.

"Tommy, you're alive."

"And so are you," he said. "Listen to me. You are in serious danger. I have your half of the score—but you'll have to come to me to collect it. The Preachers are probably watching you right now, hoping you'll lead them to me, so I need you to shake them off before we meet. Don't bring anyone else with you. Come to the place with the thing and the thing. Be there noon tomorrow."

"Tommy, I'm running out of time. I've only got 35 hours left. Can't we meet sooner?"

"That ain't possible. Noon. The thing and the thing. You know where, right?"

"Yeah," I said. "See you there."

I hung up.

"Well?" Brandon said. "What'd you find out?"

Just then a grenade came through the kitchen window. There was loud bang and an intense flash. I would have been killed again if it had been filled with explosives—but it was a stun grenade, designed to disorientate, not kill. Maria and Brandon clutched at their heads in pain—but I had already flicked on my system overrides, making the world slow down. I was blocking the pain receptors in my eyes and ears so I could function in a combat mode – diving to grab Brandon's gun as the kitchen door burst open and a massive biker appeared with a shotgun. He registered surprise when I shot him in the face. His blood sprayed out as I raced past him, spotting a second biker behind him. He moved faster than the first one, like he had overclocked himself. His swift movements surprised me. He punched me and knocked me back into the kitchen. I fired a bullet at him, but he dodged it. He attacked again. Our fists and feet blurred. I rammed his head through a wall, leaving pieces of his skull behind. The chassis of his metal skull shone through the wound. So he was a military version of me. He elbowed me in the chest. The impact knocked into the stove. He advanced. I picked up a pan and smashed it into his face. He leered.

"Nice try," he said, launching more attacks. I defended myself, deflecting his blows, knowing I'd lose if I let the fight go on much longer. Warnings were flashing about internal damage and temperature overloads. My hand was burning—so I used it to set his hair on fire. Momentarily distracted, he didn't see me picking up a carving knife until it was slamming into his forehead, puncturing his cyber implants. He dropped lifeless.

Brandon and Maria started coming around from the stun grenade. I was glad to see the violent battle had not harmed them, but it had harmed me. My right hand was blackened and I was twitching involuntarily. SYSTEM ERROR. SYSTEM ERROR.

I staggered to the bathroom and stood under the shower, hands shaking as I tried to turn on the cold water. I felt the handle turn and felt the water plunging down, steaming when it hit my head.

I woke some time later. I was in the back of a van with my clothes on, covered in packs of ice. Brandon was there, holding my burnt hand. Maria was driving.

Brandon sighed. "What did you do, Maggie?"

"I overclocked myself," I said. "Looks like I lost you the deposit."

"Are you all right?"

"I'm functional. Where are we?"

"We had to get out of there before the cops arrived. This van belongs to a friend of Maria."

One of my eyes would not show me a retinal display. That was a bad sign. The other was working fine, though. I had less than 24 hours. I doubted this body would last that long, considering the system damage. The ice had reduced my core temperature.

"Tommy gave the location of the meet. I have to get there by noon. I'm supposed to go alone – but I don't think I can drive there myself."

"We'll go with you," Brandon said.

Maria nodded. "Mija, we're staying with you."

I sat up and moved into the passenger seat. "There's a place in the desert about seventy miles from Vegas. It's a little town where we fought a battle during the Downfall. I'll give you the directions."

We drove all night and stopped only to refuel and rest. Maria and Brandon took turns driving. I rested in the back with ice packs on my body until we were close to the destination. "Tommy won't show if you are there, Brandon. Stay in the van with Maria, okay? I'll come back after seeing him."

Luckily for me, I was capable of walking. I left Brandon and Maria parked a few miles from the town, which was in a valley that had been totally destroyed during the war. The "thing and the thing" were two lumps of rocks made out of melted tanks. They looked uncannily like human hands reaching up into the sky. I could see them on the ground below, in the middle of a street of derelict, broken buildings, as I climbed down the hill, ignoring the system warnings in my head. I reached the bottom with the sun blazing down.

It was ten minutes to noon.

There was no sign of Tommy.

I waited. Noon came.

Nothing.

Had I been stood up?

I heard a buzzing.

A phone. I found it under a rock. "Hello?"

"Your half of the money is in a suitcase behind the rock behind you."

I located the suitcase and opened it. I gasped at the amount of money inside. "This is all mine?"

"Yeah," Tommy said. "You earned it. I'm just sorry everything went wrong."

"Tell me what happened."

"I had a guy working for me. An unhappy prospect for the Rebel Preachers. He told me where they had their stash house. All of their money from the border deals was stored there. He needed some ex-military people to help him break in and steal it. His name was Eli Kidder. He supplied the info and you and I went in and robbed the money. All went well – until Kidder got greedy. He wasn't happy with his third. He ambushed us at the meet. He killed you, but I got away with the money. As revenge, I called the MC to tell them Kidder was in on it. Payback for what he did to you. I heard they found him and killed him really slow. I'm so sorry I got you involved in it, Maggie. I knew I shouldn't have trust that gum-chewing weirdo. He was a devious creep."

"Wait a second. What was that about gum-chewing?"

"He was always chewing gum and leaving the wrappers on the floor of my car. Why?"

"Brandon doesn't chew gum."

"What?" Tommy said.

"Got to go. Your abuelita's in danger. She's in a van with Brandon, but it's not Brandon. It's the man who killed him."

I grabbed the suitcase and ran up the hill, reaching the top with my core temperature in the red zone, warnings flashing. Brandon and Maria were waiting for me.

"You got the money?" Brandon said.

"Yeah," I said, flicking open the case, throwing the money into the air. "Catch and release!"

A cloud of dollars filled the air between us. Brandon growled and pulled his gun. I used the distraction to charge forward at blistering speed, powering into Brandon, knocking him off his feet. I brought my fist down on his face like a piston, pounding him until my arm seized up.

He was dead.

"Maggie!" Maria cried. "What are you doing?"

"That man wasn't Brandon. Brandon was killed and his murderer put his own brain into a lookalike body. He's been fooling me this whole time, hoping I'd lead him to Tommy and the money. The real Brandon – my husband – must be in the stacks, waiting to be brought back to life. I think this money will be enough for both of us to have new bodies and new lives, providing you can pay off our debts for me. This doll is about to deactivate. Can you promise to bring me back, abuelita?"

"Don't worry, mija. I can do that for you."

I grinned and sat down, feeling my systems shutting down. I closed my eyes and pictured a better world. I just hoped I wouldn't wake up as a blonde.

***

©2019 John Moralee

Folie à Deux

Mandi Jourdan

Drew wiped the bloody blowback off the silver barrel of his pistol with the microfiber cloth he always carried from one hit to the next. His last mark had fought harder than he'd expected, but a point-blank shot to the head had been more than enough to do the job.

When he'd told Vince down at Caedis that he'd lined up two hits back-to-back, Vince had told him he was crazy. But Drew didn't have a guild like Caedis backing him—he was on his own, and he'd be damned if he missed the chance to pull two paychecks in one day. He couldn't afford to stay in one place long enough to pick up steadier work. The police would be on his ass if he wasn't careful. If he wasn't smart. Besides, Drew hadn't met a mark he couldn't handle within the first minute.

For the day's first target, he'd had a full name, an address, a date and time when the target would be home, and the contact information of his employer. For the second, he had a location—a run-down apartment where Ninth Avenue met Fifty-Second Street—along with a vague description and a first name for his target. Hathor. He'd recognized that name from somewhere, and a quick internet search had told him it belonged to an Egyptian goddess.

Great, he'd thought. *Can't even be her real name.*

Normally, he would've skipped town and ghosted his employer if he'd been given so little to go on. But $500,000 for one hit was too much to pass up, even with the risk of going in blind. With that kind of money, he could pay off his gambling debts and slow down for a while.

He tossed the blood-soaked cloth into the floorboard of his rented hovercar and slipped his pistol into his jacket pocket. He'd parked across the street from the apartment building, and when he climbed out of the car, he fell in with a crowd of commuters at the intersection, using them for cover as he crossed. He'd never been so thankful for the din of Brooklyn traffic at rush hour. He almost never took jobs in such densely populated areas, but he was counting on the constant honking of the multiple layers of hovercar traffic to cover the sound of his pistol firing. He only needed enough time for one good shot, and then he would be out of here.

Drew climbed the three steps to the front door and tried the knob. It didn't budge. There was a rusty metal keypad set into the wall beside the door, and he knew the lockpick in his jeans pocket would be useless.

"Fuck it," he muttered. A glance over his shoulder told him that no one was paying attention to what he was doing, but he had to make this fast. He pressed as close to the keypad as he could and opened his jacket, pulling his pistol free and firing a plasma bolt into the panel. The metal sizzled, and the red light at the top of the keypad went out. Drew tried the doorknob again, and when it turned, he rushed inside and slammed the door behind him. He didn't want to know whether anyone had heard the shot.

I can still be in and out before they do anything about it.

He rushed up the stairs to the second floor. Apartment 22. The door was painted white, and chips of color had flaked off to reveal the brown wood underneath.

This door opened on the first try. He flung it back, one hand shooting beneath his jacket for the grip of his pistol as he took in the sight of the woman standing in front of him. His target.

The vague description he'd received from his employer hadn't begun to capture her. She was statuesque with glossy red hair that fell down her back, and there was something wrong with her eyes. They stared straight through him like if she looked at him long enough, she might melt him into a puddle on the floor. As she watched him in a mute challenge, he thought she almost looked amused.

He pulled his pistol free and fired at her heart. She slid out of the way more quickly than he'd ever seen anyone move.

Android?

The plasma bolt burned a hole in the wooden wall where she'd just been. Drew whipped around, following her movement, and fired a second shot that she dodged just as easily. It hit a stack of plates on the kitchen counter and shattered them in a mess of porcelain that rained onto the white carpet.

He could feel his pulse in his temples, now. He might've been able to count on one shot going unnoticed long enough for him to escape, but two? Three, at least—he hadn't even hit her yet.

Then all at once, the woman was at his side, twisting his right arm behind his back so hard he was sure his bones were going to crack. He cried out and clenched his teeth, angling his wrist in her grasp, trying to aim at any part of her he could reach. When he fired, he heard her hiss and felt her grip slack, and he turned his head just enough to see that he'd hit her below her right knee. The scent of metal hit his nose, but it was too clean to be from real blood. Too sweet. The red liquid dripping from her wound was too thin, and beneath her singed skin, he saw silver.

Before Drew had time to formulate a more coherent thought, she grabbed him by the back of the neck and slammed him down onto the coffee table. The glass shattered beneath him, and his mind took a moment to register the viciously sharp pain surging through his chest, stomach, and arms from where the shards had broken skin.

Between the adrenaline and the mind-numbing pain, he found it hard to process why he was moving until the world around him shifted and he found himself lying on his back in a pile of shattered glass, his skin slick with warm blood, staring up at the flame-haired woman. She held the muzzle of his gun about an inch from his forehead. He couldn't remember dropping it.

Something sparked inside her wound. Still, she was the most beautiful thing he'd ever seen.

"Start talking," she snarled.

*

Hathor watched him, the grip of the pistol digging into her palm, her leg burning. The heat of blood trickled down her calf, and she felt it tracing a line down to her heel. The man was in worse shape—fragments of the coffee table stuck out of his chest, his arms, his neck. He was watching her with his jaw clenched. Fear lurked in his eyes, but he didn't seem willing to acknowledge it or to give her what she'd asked for.

She didn't have time to play games with him. As soon as she'd heard that Ra and Bastet had both been targeted, she'd known it would only be a matter of time until the rest of their group found themselves in the Division's crosshairs. Bastet

75

had slit the throat of the man sent after her, but Ra hadn't been as lucky. Hathor had seen pictures of him lying in the middle of a street in Washington, D.C., after his killer had fled. If this man had been sent to kill her, the Division knew where she was, and her apartment wasn't safe anymore.

She heard the impression of whispering from the couple next door, too low for the human ear at this distance, and she wondered whether her neighbors had already called the police.

Keeping the gun's muzzle between the man's eyes, she crouched. Her shin screamed in protest, bolts of pain shooting up past her knee, and she wondered exactly what the plasma had damaged within her. With her free hand, she reached for a piece of glass that stuck out of the man's shoulder and through a rip in his black shirt. In one quick motion, she twisted the cold, bloody shard, digging into as much of his skin as she could as she pulled it out.

The man screamed. Hathor dropped the glass to the carpet and pressed the gun closer, touching the skin between brown irises. There was a small freckle in the left one. The man wasn't symmetrical like she'd been built to be. She wondered how his face would shift if she fired. If he would have time to react at all, or if the light would simply leave his eyes as the plasma seared into his brain.

"Who hired you?" she asked him.

"I don't know."

A short, sharp laugh rolled from her throat. "If you want to do this the hard way, I don't mind." She pressed the gun's muzzle tighter against his skin and felt the bone beneath pushing back. Her eyes remained on his as her fingers skimmed over his chest, and she found another piece of glass just beside where the first one had been. She pushed the fragment in deeper and then pulled it out at an angle, and she looked away from his face just long enough to see a small stream of blood pour out of the wound where she'd torn it open further. When she returned her focus to his eyes, there were tears at their corners.

"Do you think I'm stupid?" His voice was tight and rough. His eyes crossed for an instant as he looked to the gun. "If I knew, I—I'd tell you."

"What did they promise you?"

"Half a million."

Hathor's lips twitched. She wondered whether that was what it had cost the Division to make her or whether it was simply all they planned to waste on disposing of her.

"What did they tell you about me?" she pressed.

"An address, a first name, and a price."

She remembered overhearing the scientists argue about what to do with her and the others. They'd said the androids weren't close enough to human. Didn't know right from wrong. Would never belong in human society. Belong *anywhere.* She'd suspected someone would come for her, but the betrayal still made her stomach churn.

Hathor gritted her teeth and pulled the gun back from the man's head slowly. A red ring colored his skin where the muzzle had been. He let out a breath and closed his eyes. Next door, the neighbors had gone silent.

She stood, took aim at the man's right foot, and fired. The shot rang in her ears, much too loud. The man screamed again and jerked his leg upward, looking at the place where the plasma had burned a hole in his leather shoe and through his skin.

"Are we even now?" the man snapped. Tears slid down his temples and into his hair.

Hathor shook her head as she turned away from him and started for the window. Glass crunched beneath the heels of her boots. "You came here to kill me, not to shoot me in the leg. You being bad at your job doesn't mean we're even." She pulled back a white gauze curtain and peered out onto the street below. A police car had just pulled up to the curb—a blue-uniformed man climbed out of it and into the crowd gathering on the sidewalk. People pointed up toward Hathor's floor. As the officer looked up, she let the curtain fall and turned back to the man lying on the shattered coffee table. His leg was still bent so that he could hold his injured foot, and his eyes were closed, his breathing heavy.

It would be so easy to leave him here. To let the police find him after she'd gone and assume that he was the reason she'd vanished. Maybe they'd think he'd killed her.

But then she wouldn't be able to use him. So far, the only contacts she had were the others like her, who couldn't afford to stay in one place for too long or make connections outside of their group, if they wanted to stay alive. This man clearly had some idea of what he was doing; she hadn't realized he was coming for her until she'd heard his footsteps outside, and he'd burst into her apartment without hesitation. He was a good shot. If she'd been human, she wouldn't have been able to move out of the way in time, and his first plasma bolt would've hit her heart. The Division was looking for its seven androids. It wouldn't be looking for a human assassin, especially one it had considered expendable enough to send after her without even enough information to keep himself safe.

This is probably a terrible idea. But I need time to think, and we're out of time here.

Hathor knelt beside the man, moving carefully to minimize her contact with the broken glass. She still felt it nick several places along her leg below the hemline of her dress, and she bit the inside of her cheek against the sting. The man's eyes snapped open. He jerked away from her, but she grabbed his wrist firmly.

"Two choices," she said. "I could leave you here for the cops to find. Or you could come with me and maybe stay out of prison for a little while longer."

Gingerly, the man lowered his leg to the floor. "Where are we going?" he asked.

*

As soon as the two entered Drew's living room, Hathor dropped him roughly onto one end of the couch. His foot hit the ground too hard, and a hiss broke through his teeth as pain splintered up to his ankle.

Should've listened to Vince and quit while I was ahead. Two hits in one day had been a terrible idea. Drew had been off his game when he'd arrived at Hathor's, and now he'd fucked up worse than he'd imagined he could. She'd demanded he take her back to his apartment, and at the risk of being shot again, he'd agreed. Now, though, as she walked a perimeter around the room and studied the photos on the walls, he knew he should've just let her kill him. She stared for several seconds too long at the picture hanging over the bar—Drew with his smiling mother at his high school graduation, three years before she'd died—and her long, slender fingers skimmed over the glass bottles of tequila and whiskey lined up along the bar's marble surface. She was studying him without asking a single question. He had to even the playing field.

"Why would someone want you dead?"

At his words, she paused, her fingertips hovering just above the mouth of a bottle of his favorite scotch.

"That's not how this is going to work," she said. She grabbed the bottle and pulled out the cork. "I don't owe you information."

"What'd you do, steal diamonds from your sugar daddy?"

Hathor rolled her eyes. She flicked the cork at him, and it drilled so hard into one of the glass fragments still sticking out of his arm that he had to close his eyes against the pain. He felt a gust of air sweep past him, and then the couch beside him shifted and squeaked. When he opened his eyes, she was sitting just to his left. She took a long drink from the bottle and propped her feet on the ottoman in front of his seat. Her bloody calf stared up at him.

I should've kept shooting until I hit somewhere more vital.

A sweet, heady scent hit his nose. Iron, lilies, and something dark and salty, like the bottom of the sea. He looked up from her calf, his eyes sliding over the hem of the green dress that fell to her knees. Her legs were thin and smooth but had been strong enough to propel her across Brooklyn at a car's pace. He'd clung to her as she'd carried him the few miles across the city, and the same intoxicating smell had filled his nose while he'd been slung over her back, holding on for his life. He wondered what her skin felt like.

"Do you really think I need a sugar daddy?"

He blinked as she spoke, heat rushing to his cheeks when he realized he'd been staring at her legs. "No," he said.

She took another swig from the bottle and passed it to him. An image of it breaking over her head flicked through his mind—the amber liquid dripping into her eyes long enough for him to retrieve the gun she'd left on the bar. Maybe the glass would splinter into her scalp and they would be one step closer to even.

He took a long gulp of scotch. His throat burned as the liquid slid down, and a tingling sensation settled at the back of his head. Hathor reached over and plucked a piece of glass from his chest with each hand. Drew choked on the scotch, the burning spreading up through his nose.

"What the hell?" he rasped through coughs.

"Focus on the alcohol. We need to get the glass out of you. Close your eyes if you can't handle looking at it."

He gritted his teeth and stared at the swirls of white paint on the ceiling. He felt his skin tear with each shard she worked free of it, and then he heard the pieces clink against the hardwood floor as one. Slowly, he lowered his gaze to look at her. She was watching him, a red brow raised, and he understood why her eyes had looked strange to him when he'd entered her apartment. They were too bright a green to belong to a human. Whoever had made her had clearly been trying for perfection, and Drew wondered whether this small distinction had been accidental or made on purpose. Had they decided she was already close enough to a Greek statue that it didn't matter if her eyes weren't realistic, or had they focused so much on the fullness of her lips that they hadn't spared enough time to fix her eyes?

"Thanks," he said flatly. "I mean, you wouldn't have had to help me if you hadn't put me through your coffee table in the first place, but—"

"You tried to kill me." She pried his fingers from where they were clenched around the bottle's neck and took a drink from it before setting it on the floor. "Listen. This is how it's going to work. I'm going to check with my friends about what we should do with you."

Drew frowned. "There are more of you? More that are wanted?"

"Yes. You're going to stay here until I get back, and if we decide you'd be an asset to us, I expect you to come with me wherever I go next."

He glanced down at the bloody glass littering the floor, and when he inhaled too deeply, his chest throbbed where his skin had ripped. "What use could I possibly be to you?" he asked.

Hathor sighed. She leaned back and rested her head against the couch, staring out over the bar. "The people who want me dead probably aren't going to stop trying. If I had someone like you, someone who could infiltrate them and help us stay two steps ahead…" She trailed off as something like pain flashed across her face. "It would be nice to have someone on my side who wasn't built to be there."

Drew blinked. Before he could respond, Hathor stood and nudged the glass out of the way with her black boot. She started for the front door.

"You'll be here when I get back," she said. Her tone had grown hard again, and she didn't look at him as she opened the door and shut it behind her.

Drew reached for the bottle of scotch. Pain shot through the upper half of his body. He abandoned the bottle and pulled off his shredded shirt, dropping it onto the spot Hathor had vacated beside him. As he surveyed his cuts, he quickly lost count of them. His chest and arms were smeared with red, and as he flexed his fingers, he felt the ghost of her grip on his wrist, when his bones had almost broken in her hands.

"The hell I will," he muttered.

*

The police car was still parked on the curb. At the sight of it, Hathor slowed from the superhuman speed with which she'd crossed Brooklyn. She forced herself to move down the sidewalk casually, ignoring the strength that pulsed through her in favor of blending in. She'd caught several confused looks from the humans she'd whipped past on the way here, but at the worst, they would think she was a Genesis android. A commercial model. If the Division had her address, though, she needed to be more careful here.

She replayed the instructions she'd given the human man in her mind. *When did I become comfortable giving orders?* Ra had been her group's leader, and since his death, Osiris seemed poised to take over that position. He'd been the one to tell her she had to lie low, to stay in her apartment as much as possible until they could learn what their creators' plan was. She'd obeyed. She'd stayed inside except when she'd

83

had to meet one of the others, and the assassin had burst through her door anyway.

"Presenting the future of robotics technology," said a smooth female voice. "The ninth generation Adam and Eve from Genesis Tech."

Hathor turned toward the screen behind the glass of the store window to her right. A woman with black hair and a blond man smiled at her from the display, wearing matching gray suits. The woman's nose was dotted with freckles, and the man's smile was slightly lopsided. Their eyes were a shade of blue Hathor had passed many times on the street, and even as she stared at the pair and scrutinized the sharp angles of their faces, she couldn't find a visual cue that they weren't human.

"Coming this fall to all major Genesis locations," said the announcer's voice.

In the glass, Hathor saw another face. This one was familiar—Horus was olive-skinned with the same too-bright green irises she saw in her own reflection. She turned to face him, and his arms wound around her, pulling her close. Her face met his shirt. She breathed in the scent of spearmint and gasoline.

"I thought—" His voice hitched on the word, and she shook her head against his chest, closing her eyes.

"I'm fine," she said.

"The ninth-generation base models can be yours starting at the unbelievable price of $50,000."

"Your leg's bleeding."

"Models with more advanced functionality vary in price. Check your local Genesis location for details."

"I'll deal with it later," said Hathor. "I need to talk with you about something." She pulled back and looked at Horus, ignoring the chatter of the humans filling Ninth Avenue and Fifty-Second Street. He was watching her warily. His copper hair reflected the light of the streetlamps. "I didn't kill the assassin."

He frowned, folding his arms across his chest. "Why not?"

"What if we can use him?"

"Hathor—"

"Think about it," she pressed, pulling Horus closer to the window and away from the people walking along the sidewalk. "The Division is looking for us. Just us. What if we had someone like *them* on our side? What if we had a human spy?"

"He just tried to *kill* you. Do you think he's going to suddenly want to work for you?"

Hathor glanced to the screen as the Genesis models smiled at her once more before the commercial ended. The assassin had been offered ten times the price of one of those androids to take her down. He'd certainly tried. But while she'd sat beside him drinking scotch, he'd looked at her in a way she hadn't anticipated. There had been lust in his eyes as they'd roved her legs, not malice.

"I think he can be persuaded," she said, looking back to Horus. He held her gaze silently, and when his lips twisted in disdain, she knew he understood.

"Is that what you want?" he asked. "Some human asshole who tried to shoot you?"

Hathor laid her hands on Horus's shoulders and pulled him down to her. He didn't resist, though his eyes narrowed. She pressed her lips

85

to his. His skin was warm, and when she felt him sigh and his fingers slid into her hair, she could almost pretend that they stood here under different circumstances. She could imagine that they had met and fallen in love however humans did—bumped into each other on the street, accidentally hailed the same cab, grown up next door to one another.

Instead, when Horus rested his hand on her arm, she remembered when he'd done the same in Dahab, when they'd paused outside the home of one of the men the Division had sent them to kill. Horus had told her she was beautiful, and when their target had shot at her head, Horus had caught the plasma bolt in his bare hand and snapped the man's neck. When their group had returned to the Division's base and reported that they'd taken the initiative to destroy all of Dahab to keep the threat from spreading, Horus had stepped closer to Hathor, and she'd known he'd made the same observation she had—that their creators had gone white as sheets and that a few of them had reached for their weapons. He'd taken her hand as they'd run away, and even when they were both supposed to be lying low in separate New York boroughs, they took turns breaking cover to see one another.

The assassin hadn't seen her kill civilians and set fire to houses. He'd still looked at her the same way Horus did.

Hathor pulled back and rested her forehead against Horus's. "I want you," she said quietly. "And I want all of us to stay safe. Anything I do with the human is to make sure that happens."

"Do what you have to do." Horus withdrew his hands from her and turned away, starting down the sidewalk.

Each step sent a fresh wave of agony through Drew's foot. He limped toward the front door, the bag he'd hastily packed slung over his shoulder. He'd grabbed the essentials he'd left behind that morning; he never brought any form of identification when he went after targets, but he would need his wallet if he planned to rent a new apartment. He'd pulled the photo he'd taken with his mother at his graduation off the wall and shoved it between unfolded clothes and toiletries and bags of potato chips. He clung to his pistol, still feeling the sting of its cold muzzle where Hathor had pressed it to his forehead.

The door opened, and she stood on the threshold, a fire in her eyes he couldn't identify. His stomach lurched.

"We had a deal," she said.

Drew shook his head. "You told me what I was going to do. I never agreed."

He raised the gun and pointed it at the space between her eyes. His grip tightened as he anticipated her move. Surely she would knock it out of his hand or slide out of the way or find some other path to avoid his shot, but he had to do *something,* had to show her somehow that he was good at this job, that he she hadn't broken him. She was the first mark he'd failed to take out, and just being near her clouded his senses, made him ache, but she hadn't broken him. He could still do this. He could squeeze the trigger if he wanted to.

She stared at him, and for an instant, he could almost convince himself that she wanted him to fire. The sadness he'd seen in her inhuman eyes returned, and then it was gone as quickly as it had come.

"Aren't you tired of doing this alone?" she asked him.

She took a step forward, and the gun's muzzle met the olive skin of her forehead. She kept her eyes on his.

The gun shook in his hand. He'd been alone since his mother's death. He burned through fake identities and short leases and cars rented with cash, always alone, always running. He'd never had had anyone to run to.

He lowered his gun.

Hathor closed the distance between them and molded her body to his, one hand in his hair, one on his cheek to pull him closer. She kissed him hard, and the warm, all-consuming smell of flowers and blood and secrets he would never know filled his senses. His eyes closed. Slowly, she backed him toward the bar, and when he felt a stool against the backs of his legs, he sat, pulling her along with him. She climbed onto his lap and leaned into him, her breasts meeting his chest through the shirt he'd pulled on to replace the one she'd ruined. His hands skimmed over the smooth, warm skin of her arms, her shoulders, her back, her neck, and she felt like every fantasy he'd ever had pulled into one being. So far beyond him that he hated himself for being human.

He opened his eyes. "Yes," he breathed against her lips.

"Yes what?" Her legs wound around his waist, her skirt sliding up her thighs.

"I'll go with you. Do whatever you need."

A smile graced her lips, and when she lifted his wallet into his line of sight, he realized he didn't know when she'd unzipped his bag.

"Then Drew Morrison is going to have to die," she said. She laid the wallet on the bar behind him and pulled the gun gently from his grasp before his mind had processed her words. She rested the gun beside the wallet and pulled the bag from his shoulder, and he turned in time to see her dump its contents across the bar's marble surface.

"What are you—?"

"Drew. Sweetheart."

He felt her fingers against his chin, guiding his face back to hers. She kissed him softly and smoothed his hair back from his forehead.

"People will need to think you're dead. You're going to have to start over."

Hathor raised a silver lighter, and Drew had no idea where she'd gotten it. She felt suddenly heavier on his lap, and the smell of blood overpowered the sweetness that surrounded her. When she smiled, something twisted within him.

He stood, wincing when pain shot through his foot, and shifted her gingerly to the floor. He limped over to the couch and bent to retrieve the bottle of scotch she'd left beside it, and then he returned to the bar. Pulling in a breath so deep every one of his cuts stung, he tipped the bottle over and poured its contents across his belongings. He knew he would have to douse the whole apartment. Amber liquid pooled in the corner of the glass covering the photo, and Drew couldn't look at his mother where she stared at him from beyond it. He set the bottle on the counter beside his saturated wallet.

"Light it," he said.

***

©2019 Mandi Jourdan

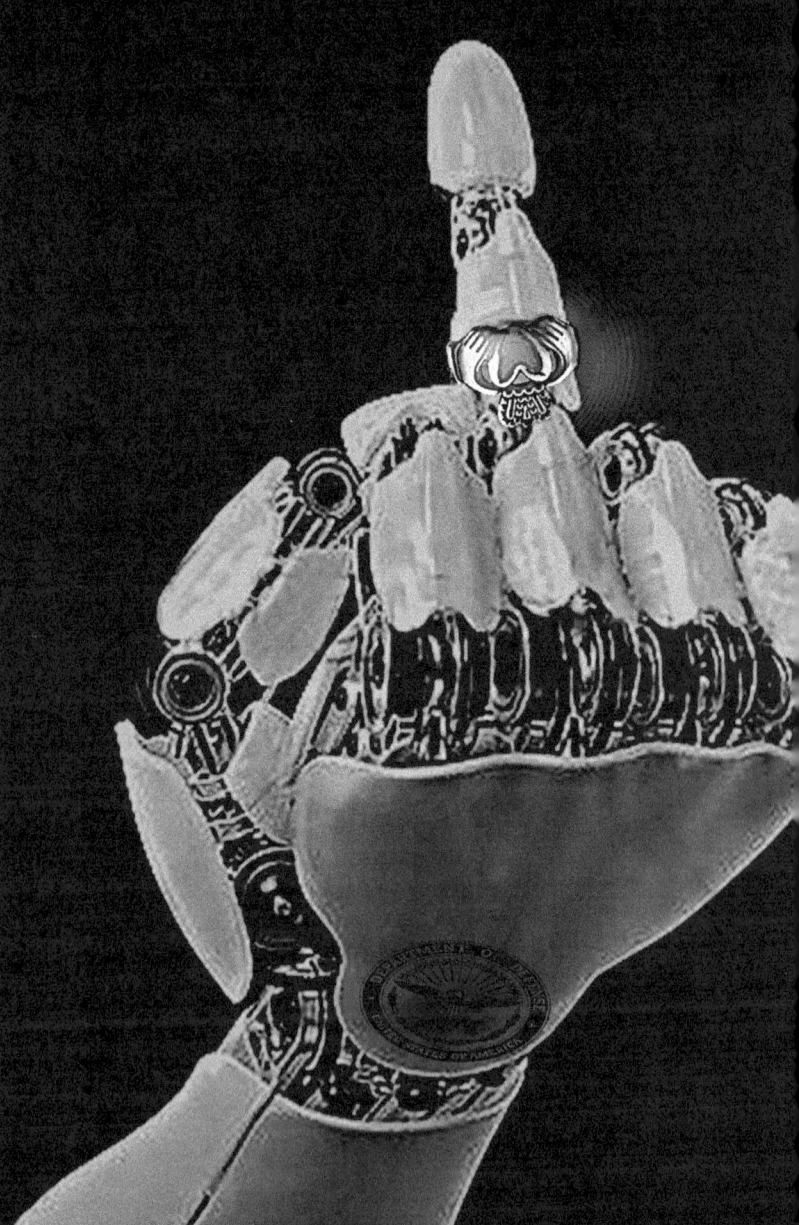

My daughter stands in the doorway and reeks of burnt metal. White wisps of smoke mark her path to my apartment. I scan the hallway in case others might be lurking, an old habit that will never die. Her eyes are gone, just two smoking holes.

"Long time no see," she says.

She braces herself against the wall and slides to the floor, the light catching her blonde hair. For a moment she is five years old and her eyes are cornflower blue.

"It wasn't easy finding you. I had o keep asking directions." She reaches out with her natural hand. "I can almost touch you, pops. I hope you still remember me."

"I remember you."

"Say my name."

"Gretchen."

Her other hand crackles with knuckle sparks. My daughter returned from the war with new eyes, one hand and maybe an ear. I've lost track. Implants aren't supposed to give out, not like this. I wonder what she's done to herself this time. I wonder what she wants.

"Pops, you need to kill someone for me." Ocular lubricant rolls down her cheeks in black, greasy tears. "Maybe more than one person. I'll pay, of course."

"I don't need your money."

"Really? Because my nose still works, and I'm betting you haven't taken a shower in weeks.

Also, something died in your kitchen. Maybe you just forgot to clean. Or forgot you had a kitchen."

If they made implants for early-stage dementia, I'd be first in line. The short-term memory goes first, so I don't remember the last time I cleaned my kitchen. But I remember my daughter lives on the street. I remember our last encounter. That's enough.

"Are you listening?"

Her hand—the one I don't trust—reaches out and grabs my throat. Telescoping fingers tighten their grip. A titanium thumb presses on my larynx, and I can feel her Claddagh ring against my skin. It represents love, loyalty and friendship.

Her voice rasps like sandpaper. "Someone is giving us bad meds. I get anti-rejection packs every month. Same prescription for years. Something's changed, and it's too late to figure out. I'm cascading, good as gone. You need to track down who's doing this and make people pay. That's what you do, right? Make people pay."

"I don't negotiate with people who threaten me."

"I am not negotiating. Do this and we'll be square. Or I'll kill you here."

My head stays perfectly still. "You said us. Someone is giving us bad meds. If this is widespread, talk to the police."

Her smile drips with spite. "You're recommending the police? That's rich. The police think we're killing ourselves. They think we're stupid."

"Christ, Gretchen. You're not stupid. All I ever wanted for you was a good life . . ."

Segmented fingers close on my neck. That thumb hammers my windpipe. Then she sighs, and her body goes limp and she's gone. Just like that she's gone. Except her hand doesn't let go. The damn thing is stuck, and now I can't breathe. I dig my fingers into those two black eye holes and come away with lubricant mixed with viscera. I smear the steaming mess all over my neck and slowly slide free. A lock of blonde hair falls across her face, and I instinctively curl it behind her ear. Then it hits me what just happened. A sudden burst of grief topples me like a punch to the liver. My daughter coughed up her last moments like a seized engine and no one can fix her. But I've got a little time.

Do this and we'll be square.
Maybe I can track it down.

*

The cops send a drone. By the time it arrives, I've covered my daughter with an old beach blanket. We spent our best days on the sand, watching the stealth destroyers sailing from Norfolk in their tumble-down hulls, looking like they'd sink any minute. Gretchen always wanted to swim out and hop aboard.

"Take off the towel," says the drone operator.

Drone operators are either young or old. This one sounds like a kid. He's back at the station,

93

probably jerking off between assignments and wolfing down handfuls of blue scoots. The drone isn't a threat, either. It's a simple one-eyed scanner, unarmed and unable to interface with courts to swear out search warrants.

It hovers over her black eyes, then scans her wrist chip. "Gretchen Barnes," the operator says. "Last known residence was Southeast Municipal Shelter. Looks like another suicide."

"Another?"

"Maybe an accidental overdose. These veterans don't maintain their prescriptions and buy stuff off the street. Once the body starts rejecting implants, it's over. You're all metaled up with no place to go." He chuckles. "She served in the 369th out of Fort Armistead. God knows what she went through."

The drone elevates to my eye level. "You're her dealer?"

"Her father."

A warm light scans my neck. "Looks like she tried to strangle you. Some father."

"I want an autopsy. My daughter said someone was giving her bad meds. She said it's happened to others. This needs to be investigated as a suspicious death, maybe even a homicide."

"Sure, grandpa. We'll drop everything and get on that. Have you checked the suicide rate of first-gen implanted veterans? I did a paper on it. And look in the mirror. Your daughter lived on the street and you didn't do shit. Now she's dead and here comes the guilt train. Hold up your wrist, old man." He scans my ID chip and falls silent.

"Something wrong, officer?"

"You're Custer Barnes."

"Correct."

"From the Hampton Roads Amalgamated Construction Council. Vice president of security"

"Retired."

"Arrested fourteen times on charges ranging from simple assault to murder. Charges dropped in all cases. You're *that* Custer Barnes."

"Does my daughter get an autopsy or not?" I lunge at the drone and it pulls it back, almost smashing into the wall. "Made you flinch."

"Look, Mr. Barnes. I'm just a summer intern."

"Yes. I hear you did a paper once."

"An autopsy request is above my pay grade. I perform an initial assessment and send a unit. They'll transport your daughter directly to the funeral home. It'll be Powers Mortuary. He handles all the first-gen implants. Gotta go."

The drone retreats until it smashes through the window at the end of the hallway. I smile as it drops out of sight. After all this time, I still scare people.

*

Jerry Powers and I rammed around as kids. We swam in the bay and took day trips to the Newport News shipyard as those giant hulls rose from the dry dock in glorious Navy gray. The sun warmed our backs and we traded stories about places we'd visit, the money we'd make. Jerry's

95

stories were always more grandiose. In truth, he was kind of a dick.

The mortuary is a 15-minute walk, but I order a scat to avoid the July heat. It leaves me off in front of a laminate brick building with smoked glass. The door slides open and cold air washes over me. Jerry stands there as if I'm expected. Maybe I called ahead.

"Hey, Cuss. Sorry about your daughter." He wears a seersucker suit and white bucks, playing the part of a bourbon-sipping Virginia gentleman living in a country house with a wrap-around porch. But those darting eyes belong in a pawnshop in a bad part of town.

"Jerry. Glad you're handling the funeral."

He waves a hand. "Veterans benefits automatically cover costs of alkaline hydrolysis, so no problem. I'm sure you've got a spot picked out. From what I gather, Gail was on borrowed time."

"Her name was Gretchen."

He checks his handheld. "My bad. Where will she go?"

"In the Hampton cemetery. Next to her mother."

Jerry puts away his handheld and looks at the floor. He starts to laugh, as if some embarrassing joke materialized from the tiles and started dancing around. "In-ground burials haven't been a thing for years. With alkaline hydrolysis, you end up melting in the backyard. Everyone thinks it's poetic if grandma fertilizers your vegetable garden. We'll remove the implants, of course. She's got titanium, graphite, Lord knows what else." He goes to his desk and calls up a screen. "I see her eyes failed."

"Spectacularly."

"That's too bad. WDVs show no mercy." His eyes go soft. "I'll contact her unit up at Fort Armistead. I've buried a few from there. All suicides."

Something sparks in my brain. A frayed synapse reconnects. "Wait, no. Gretchen didn't kill herself. And it wasn't an accident. She told me."

He looks at the far wall and seems to sort through possible responses before settling on one. "I assume you're taking medication for your dementia."

"How the hell did you know . . .?"

He puts both hands on my shoulders. "You told me three weeks ago at the farmer's market. You were getting cheese and bread and I scolded you for not buying more vegetables. You said something about counseling sessions."

I remember the visit to the farmer's market and vaguely recall seeing Jerry. He might have asked about Gretchen. I wonder how many others I've told. The doctor gave me medication to slow the brain rot, but it's not a cure. The automated counselor pissed me off, so what Jerry says sounds about right. Talking to a robot is no way to die. After that first session, I cleaned my old gun and decided to keep it handy.

"I was thinking Wednesday for the service," Jerry says. "Miles does the day-to-day stuff now, so it's his call. He's working his other job at the moment."

"Your son is old enough to handle the business?"

"He's forty-three." Jerry looks at me with something resembling pity, and he needs to stop acting like I'm his next customer or I'll clock him. Melt into the backyard my ass. I'll throw Gretchen in the Chesapeake Bay before that happens.

"Gotta go, Jerry."

Back at my apartment, a package from the city Community Services Department sits outside my door. Gretchen's things. The box is no bigger than an overnight bag and it's not even half full. She has a veteran benefits card, a few energy biscuits, a dead handheld and some clothes tied up in a roll. The most interesting thing is a thumb disc. I'm thinking it's her DD-214 discharge papers and other military records, but when I put it onscreen, up pops 50 files.

Do I even want to look?

Yeah, I do.

*

File 1: Her swearing-in ceremony back in '48. Gilda and I attended as proud parents. Images of us holding hands and locking arms. I remember thinking how it was worth it, all the bad things I did. She was on her way to a better life.

File 6: Gretchen in is Turkey. Probably her third or fourth duty station. The sharp angles of her face testify to her transformation. No baby fat, no smiles. She's outside the wire on a foot patrol. Micronesia is on everyone's mind. Unruly oligarchs have ousted American business interests and killed a few of us in the process. Micronesia scares no one: a cake walk against a disorganized and poorly armed opponent. Isn't that how it always starts?

By File 23: Three years later. Gretchen paces in a jungle clearing, surrounded by a few dozen men and women. Her voice is clipped and precise, a tone I never knew she possessed. She describes a mechanized Marine unit that came across aural mines. It destroyed their eardrums in less than two minutes. She tells them to keep antibiotics injectors within easy reach until someone figures this out. The term Weaponized Designer Virus had yet to enter the lexicon. When her grunts start bitching about fighting in chem suits, Gretchen holds up a finger and they fall silent. Stay in battle rhythm. Pins and needles, people.

File 49: A year has passed. Gretchen sits on the ground, blindfolded, making a personal log entry. Losing her eyes was like getting a pie in the face. Wipe away the pudding and your fingers go into two holes. The lack of pain is what scares her.

File 50: Post war. Gretchen drinks at a table with her buddies. They stare at a stack of empties. The jittery stress of the jungle persists. It remains a living, breathing thing that haunts their faces. A big man next to Gretchen downs two mugs of beer in succession. The joke goes up: His leg is hollow. Gretchen bear-hugs the man, then reaches down and comes away with his left leg up to mid-thigh. She holds up the implant and frowns: "This is definitely hollow, first sergeant. Peg legs violate the rules of engagement."

She squeezes the upper thigh. The knee cocks.

"Captain don't . . ."

The leg kicks on its own. It jumps from Gretchen's hand and shatters several mugs on the bar. Everyone drops to the floor and comes up drenched in beer. For a second, they act like an attack is imminent. Then come howls of laughter, a cathartic release of tension. Gretchen puffs herself up.

"First sergeant, please explain why your leg is homicidal."

The first sergeant, a thick-necked sort with flat nose, stands up straight. "It's a hard flex, ma'am. I was kick-boxing the heavy bag before I came here. When it's detached, you can work the knee manually with a good squeeze and it will execute its most recent movement."

"You're saying the leg remembers."

"After a fashion, yes ma'am."

Gretchen fixes the sergeant with a cold stare. "Your leg is hereby demoted for kicking a superior officer. But Jesus Christ on a stick, sergeant, I never knew that shit. For making me a smarter officer, I owe you a beer."

The final item in her bag is a business card. It's from the walk-in clinic where she received her prescriptions. The name on the card is Miles Powers and for some reason it sounds familiar.

Wait. Miles is Jerry's son.

*

The Jarvis-Frazier Free Clinic is perilously near old downtown, an area that surrendered to rising sea levels a decade ago. A scat drops me near the clinic and I begin to shamble forward, pulling at my clothes. My dementia dance is a work in progress, but it's improving. Soon I'll be doing it full time and not pretending. I shuffle behind the clinic to a loading dock, then into a supply room where I pretend to see things. When I knock over a stack of boxes, a young man in surgical scrubs bursts into the room.

"Did you come from the dorm?"

"Um, I think so."

"Back to bed."

He steers me through a maze of hallways, then into a room with about a dozen beds, half of which are occupied. A nurse moves from patient to patient, checking vitals and entering data into a handheld. A man in the nearest bed starts to sing "Take Me Back to Micronesia." He's POW-skinny and his left leg appears to be a dead implant. The nurse comes over to fuss at him and leaves her handheld on an empty bed. I drag a leg across the room and pick it up, start punching at the screen, seemingly at random. The nurse sees me and smiles. I'm just a puppy that needs regular

101

meals and a few pats on the head. I look up Gretchen's name and scan her list of meds, the record of her visits. It's all normal: generic anti-rejection drugs and routine checkups.

Too normal.

Hands settle on my shoulder and gently turn me around. There stands a grown-up Miles Powers, wearing an administrator's ID. He looks nothing like his delicate father: block-headed with a double chin, a lipless mouth and pig eyes. Ah, but pigs are smart. He knows why I'm here.

"Hello, Mr. Barnes. Dad said he talked to you. Sorry about your daughter."

"You filled out, Miles."

He forces out a laugh. "Got fat, you mean. I work in patient records now. Still deciding whether to take over the family business full time."

Gretchen's file is displayed on the handheld. Miles wags a finger at me. "That's a no-no, Mr. Barnes. We shouldn't be looking at the records of others."

"Gretchen was my daughter."

"Unless she tagged you for disclosure, I'll have to insist you stop. I'm sure her file is in order. Let me see you out."

We return to the maze of hallways. Double doors slide open. A short passageway leads to another door and Miles presses his thumb on a keypad. It slides open to reveal a darkened room, not the loading dock. He pushes me forward. His hand stays on my lower back and grabs a fistful of my shirt.

"Watch your step, Mr. Barnes. You might fall."

Really? That line? I pretend to stumble forward, then jerk back with as much youthful snap as I can muster. My head makes a satisfying crack against the bridge of his nose. I turn around and sink a knee in his stomach. As he bends over and vomits, I walk briskly away. Never run. Never show fear.

*

Back at my apartment, I reach out to Mr. Normandy on my main screen. It switches to voice-only mode.

"Welcome, Barnes," says the voice.

"You're not Mr. Normandy."

"I'm your automated counselor. Your reach-out was routed to me. Per Franklin Normandy."

"Mr. Normandy no longer takes my calls? Fuck me."

"Profanity will not assist. I can help you for the next thirty minutes. Our last conversation was eight days ago. We talked about labeling your personal items after you brushed your teeth with shaving cream. How is that going?"

"I need Mr. Normandy's clearance for a job."

"Explain further."

"I can't. It's illegal."

"Our conversation is protected by federal law, Mr. Barnes."

If Mr. Normandy has cut me loose, my days are truly numbered. He's probably worried about

103

what might spill from my mouth as I ramble around town in the coming months. But maybe he's monitoring these sessions. Maybe this will get back to him.

"Someone is killing first-generation implanted veterans and making the deaths look like drug overdoses, either intentional or accidental, including my daughter. I know who's doing it. I need to find proof, then I need to kill this person. And before you ask, the green mob doesn't go to the police."

"Explain the Green Mob."

"You don't get out much."

"Sarcasm will not assist."

I take a deep breath, count to three, exhale. "Climate change, sea level rise, the melting ice caps. What's it have in common? No, strike that. How do you fight sea level rise? Give me three examples."

"Raised structures. Diverting retention ponds. Automated flood gates."

"Very good. And they all require construction. They require contracts and bids and skilled trades. Ever since the days of pop rivets and labor unions, the mob has had it fingers in the construction industry. That's why the green mob exists. We bankroll environmental protection."

"To what end?"

"Because we love Mother Earth. And money. Not necessarily in that order."

"How does the mob achieve this purpose?"

"Jesus, dumbo, try to follow along. Let's say you bid on a job—a seawall replacement—and promise to pay skilled labor rates. You win the contract, then pull people off the street and pay half of what you promised, then use bots for the rest. But you still get full funding. All this happens with the oversight of Mr. Normandy and his associates, who awarded the contract through a shell company that deals with City Hall. It's simple."

"What is your role, Mr. Barnes?"

"Muscle. Maybe a contractor wants a larger cut than planned. Maybe someone wants to blow the whistle, or a rival contractor wants a piece of the business. I break fingers and thumbs, noses and jaws. Sometimes I kill. Shit, I truly hope you were right about this being protected."

"I am. This gives you satisfaction?"

"It paid well. I remember getting coded messages like it was yesterday. My salary was laundered through the dark cloud . . ."

"That's not what I asked, Mr. Barnes. Deflection will not assist."

"Fine, smartass. Yes, it gave me satisfaction." My hand worms between the couch cushions. "I sent my daughter to a military academy. Expensive as hell, but she graduated with honors and got a head start on a military career. It's what she always wanted and . . . she used to thank me."

"Tell me about your daughter."

"She's gone. And she still hates me."

"Why does she . . ."

I shoot the screen dead. Somehow my old gun ended up in my hand. Must have stuck it in the couch cushions.

*

My bedroom closet is a repository for old hardware, and I start digging around for a new screen to replace the one I killed. I move the laundry hamper and dirty clothes spill onto the floor, including the shirt stained with Gretchen's blood.

Of course. I'm really getting slow.

*

Finding drone boy is a snap. He's a summer intern and the police love to publicize the young men and women who represent the future of law enforcement. The Hampton Police Department has a dozen interns working this summer, according to their portal. They give each one five minutes to say a few words. I listen for the right voice, praying that my rotted synapses won't betray me. The drone operator sounds a lot like Merrick Forsythe, a junior at Old Dominion University who wants to extend the long arm of justice by flying the latest in unmanned aerial vehicles.

When Merrick comes on screen, his face turns a shade of gray. "Y-Yes sir?"

"Thought it was you. How's it going, son?"

"I don't know about the autopsy of your daughter. I filed my report and it goes into a folder with a lot of others, plus I'm not sure the

106

police would be the initial contact because I did some checking with the medical examiner and they are very . . ."

"Stop talking."

"I'm stopping. Sure."

I hold up my shirt. "Can you analyze the blood on this garment? Or arrange to have it analyzed? There must be a portable or two lying around where you are. I'm not comfortable walking into a police station, but I can send a scat your way. Then give me the results by tomorrow morning. I'm looking for drug levels of any kind."

"Consider it done, Mr. Barnes."

"Off the books?"

"Sure."

If Merrick bends over for old geezers like me, he'll never stop getting fucked. But men must learn things on their own, and now isn't the time. His balls can drop later.

*

The next morning, everyone piles into Powers Mortuary for the funeral. An active-duty contingent from Fort Armistead shows up along with veterans from Gretchen's old unit, walking stiffly in ill-fitting civilian suits. Everyone collides in a series of bear hugs. I wear the same black suit that got me through Gilda's funeral ten years ago. The old bulletin is still in the pocket, along with the results from the blood analysis.

Gretchen rests in an open casket, medals affixed to a spotless green uniform. Two photos flank her: an official military portrait and one of her in the jungle, smiling and streaked with sweat. Her expression is not that different from when she played on the beach years ago.

I caress her cold cheek and whisper. "You should have killed me when you had the chance, baby girl. Pops is about to embarrass you."

Jerry speaks first. He mentions Gilda, who worked as a public health nurse before she got sick. I choke back a sudden sob and get a few looks. *That must be the dad. The old mobster.* Then Jerry invites me up with a practiced wave of his hand. I face rows of people in straight-backed chairs.

"I lost Gretchen the other day. Then yesterday, I got pissed off at my shrink – which is a piece of outdated software—and shot it with a forty-year-old pistol. Now you know where she gets it from."

Nervous laughter.

"Let's face it: You knew Gretchen better than I did. But I can tell you a few things. I bet she never mentioned finishing third in the spelling bee, then coming home and trashing her bedroom because she didn't finish first. As consolation, I bought her a pair of cross-country skis because we had snow that year. She broke her leg racing a garbage truck. But she won."

Smiles and nods.

"But the real story is about her death. Gretchen didn't die from an accidental overdose, and it sure as hell wasn't suicide." I pull out a fistful of paper. "She wasn't taking anti-rejection

108

drugs. She was being fed the wrong medication on purpose."

A chair squeaks as Jerry gets up.

"Her records look fine, but this blood test says otherwise. She had a dangerous mix of tranquilizers and stimulants that knocked her implants out of whack. She said it was happening to others. Check your individual prescription plans. Get your blood tested."

Jerry takes my arm. He whispers something about taking a break and pulls me into another room laid out like a waiting area, with chairs and a couch arranged around a table. Miles sits on the couch, two black eyes from his broken nose. The sight gives me the warm fuzzies. Jerry shoves me forward and closes the door.

"Mr. Barnes, you shouldn't tell stories like that," Miles says.

Jerry hangs near the door. "I'll go out and tell the mourners that Mr. Barnes hasn't been himself since his daughter's death. The dementia is getting the best of him. I'll apologize and we'll move on with the service."

Miles nods. "That should work. I'll take him downstairs."

"What's downstairs?"

"The crematorium."

Never ask the question if you don't want to know the answer.

*

The crematorium sits in the far corner. It's smaller than I expected, just a door built into the wall with a simple control panel. Against the far wall are three gurneys. Two are empty, but the third holds a misshapen form under a black sheet.

"Say hello to your daughter," Miles says, nodding toward the form.

Under the sheet is a pile of implants. Arms, eyes, lower legs. A few pieces that might be inner ears. Too many for a single body. Each piece has a luminous tag with a scannable code that niggles at a dark corner of my brain. Symbols that belong to another lifetime.

"Implants should be returned to the government," I say.

Miles laughs. "How good of you to defend the rule of law."

The scannable code on each implant is a series of symbols followed by a five-digit number. It once made sense to me. It mattered a lot. I would look forward to seeing that code on a regular basis. It created . . . fuck, the dots aren't connecting. I sort through the ruined metal and then I see a hand with a Claddagh ring on a blackened thumb.

"Her ring."

"Yes. It increases the value of the implant."

Value? Of course. The symbols and the five-digit number are a financial routing tag for the Dark Cloud. That's how Mr. Normandy paid me years ago. I walk myself through it, hearing my own words. "You're killing . . . you're killing veterans and selling their implants on the black market. Titanium, graphite and other rare metals would be as profitable as gold and silver and not as traceable. You that hard up for money, Miles?"

He shrugs. "These veterans are bankrupting us. The reimbursement for the funerals hardly covers our costs. Then I go to work at the clinic and deal with their entitled demands. They weren't drafted, Mr. Barnes. They volunteered to fight. They're not my problem. And they're going to die anyway, so we might as well manage it."

"Manage it?"

The last jolt of hostility that coursed through Gretchen's body must have fused the Claddagh ring to her thumb. Miles motions me toward the crematorium, and now my daughter's honesty is my only hope. I pray that she meant to kill me.

"Hand over the implant," he says.

"Here you go."

I turn around and squeeze the wrist, initiating a hard flex. The fingers telescope and grab his throat. The titanium thumb cracks his voice box. Fingers tear through muscle and blood vessels and finally bone. It was the strangulation meant for me, the last bitter spit of rage fueled by a father's abandonment.

Good job, Gretchen.

I hope this makes us square.

***

©2019 Hugh Lessig

111

NIGHT MAYOR

Nick Kolakowski

With twenty minutes to waste before her shift began, Maxine tortured herself by pulling out her phone to check her bank balance: a whole three dollars and twenty-three cents to her name, with a big stack of bills still outstanding and five days until her next paycheck: in other words, a typical week in her awesome life.

Ever the glutton for punishment, she opened the left pocket of her tactical vest ('I DO ALL MY OWN STUNTS' stenciled across the back in red paint) and poked at the crumpled pack of Chinese cigarettes stuffed between two clips of Double-Pop ammo, feeling three smokes—far too few to see her through the day, unless she bummed three or four off Rodrigo, which would mean submitting to his questions about their non-relationship. Which was a pretty typical dilemma, too.

Want something a little more out of the ordinary? How about her higher-than-usual chances of dying in a massive fireball before noon?

Maxine believed they always needed a minimum of two escorts on a typical run. The Company deciding to strip convoy protection down to one car was corporate stupidity at its A-1 finest: some bean-counter at a comfortable desk in Lower Manhattan making a decision based on digits on a spreadsheet, as if things like margin and profit meant anything at all on the highway, with its screaming bandits and fires on the ridges.

But headquarters had no ear for her opinions, especially after she'd broken her supervisor's nose at the end of an especially bloody shift. *Man's a chump*, she told the idiots on the review board. *Besides, I saved two of the trucks, didn't I? How much money you make off that?* In the end they docked her pay twenty percent, forcing her to give up virtually everything except cigarettes and junk food and her phone bill. She slept in the backseat of the cruddy Qirui hatchback she'd owned for twelve years, which the Company—in its sadistic definition of mercy—let her park in a corner of the razor-wired Employee Lot. Who didn't like falling asleep to the soothing roar of biofuel generators?

"I guess they're tired of me," Maxine told the other drivers after she received the first solo-escort assignment. "Who's getting my locker once I'm gone?"

Fifteen minutes before convoy rollout, Maxine bought a can of bitter coffee from the machine in the depot break-room (two dollars and fifty-two cents left, her phone flashed at her) and slugged it down in a single gulp, hoping the caffeine would jump-start her dull nerves. The worst part of unending double shifts is it means your days off are never days off, because you still need to go to sleep at 2 A.M. and wake up three hours later if you want any chance of preserving your biorhythms. Keeping on that schedule made her feel like a zombie every waking minute, her thoughts swimming through gray fog, her nerves

114

like jagged glass buried just beneath the skin.

In the depot garage Maxine unlocked her personal cabinet and opened the foam-lined case where she kept her prosthetics and other equipment. She pulled up her left sleeve and peeled back the plastic strip that guarded her forearm's release lever, popped off the limb and set it in the case. Next she retrieved her Work Arm, a custom job she'd machined herself with an industrial 3D printer and some spare parts bought off an online bazaar for secondhand military hardware: ballistic composite wrapped around a steel frame and bundles of synthetic tendons, power and speed in one badass package—and unlike the commercial versions, no capacity to feel pain. Her stump buzzed as the silicon nerves joined with her brainstem in holy matrimony.

That task complete, she drew her service pistol from another section of the case, loaded it with one of the Double-Pop clips ("The quicker putter-downer!" is how they advertised the ammo on guns-and-hunting Websites), and slid it into the polymer holster strapped to her hip. Hearing Rodrigo walk up behind her, she sighed and called out, "What's up?"

"You heard of the Murder Market?" he asked.

"No. Sounds like a band." She turned to study him, so scrawny in his bulky vest and loose cargo pants, like a little boy playing war.

He held up his phone, its screen displaying an old-school Jolly Roger above a cluster of links.

"This Website. You list someone you want killed, and people donate money—maybe they throw in a few bucks, maybe a couple thousand. Whoever commits the murder, they get all the cash."

"That even slightly legal?"

"Prolly not," Rodrigo tapped the top link, and the skull-and-crossbones gave way to a long list of names and photos. "But if the dude wanting the deed done is in Beijing, the victim's in Los Angeles, and the Website's hosted off the coast of New Russia or whatever, it'd be hard for the cops in one jurisdiction to do squat about shutting it down."

"Yep, sure sounds like a huge legal mess. Why am I caring?" Maxine walked toward her escort vehicle, hoping it sent Rodrigo the message: I have places to go, things to do, fireballs to dodge.

Rodrigo kept jabbering. "Payment's in crypto-currency, so nobody knows who's ordering the hits, or donating." He flicked through names. "The killer takes that, flips it to dollars with some launderer taking ten or twenty percent for themselves, who'd know? Here, you really need to see this."

He tilted the screen, revealing Maxine's photo above her name and far too much identifying information: age, occupation, state of residence. "There's a minimum limit for a hit, and nobody's contributed enough to put you above that line, but the amount's rising. I saw it this morning."

Her prosthetic limb blurred out and snatched

116

the phone from his grip. "How'd you find this?"

He paused. "I was stalking you online. Sorry, I've been doing it since we broke up…"

"That sounds healthy." She sped down the page, to the section that listed contributors and amounts: five names, all stupid Internet handles (AngryCat55, Jack Reacher, Suave_Android, LadiesMan, Four-Pump-Chump), each donating a couple hundred dollars to her demise, none leaving a comment about it. She checked the time, realizing she had only eight minutes before the convoy arrived—barely enough to run through a vehicle check. "I gotta speak to Tony."

"Just don't bust his nose again," Rodrigo yelled as she jogged out of the garage.

II.

Tony's desk featured six widescreens stacked in two rows, aglow with video feeds from drones skimming dead valleys, trucks rumbling down the highways, the main street of a ghost town to the east. The bandage across his nose gleamed blue in the reflected light from the monitors. Maxine noted with no small pleasure that the swelling around his eyes had settled into a purple stain that would linger for weeks.

"Why should I care what's on some Website?" he snapped.

Maxine grinned. "Isn't the safety and welfare of employees the company's chief concern?"

Tony glanced at the truck monitor. "Convoy's

117

six minutes out. You don't get on the road, you won't be an employee."

"This Website threat qualifies as hazard pay, I think."

He settled back in his plush command chair, hands folded on the soft mound of his stomach, a vein in his forehead ticking overtime. "You know I got no control over pay."

She lingered on the screens, losing herself in the rough symphony of machines in movement. The sight of all that technology, and the thought that her skills would help it survive, made her a little proud of her job. "Maybe you're the one who put my name on that Website."

His jaw dropped. "You accusing me?"

Her grin trembled at the edges. "Sure, why not? Besides, if I file the complaint, you know Corporate will start digging. You still taking kickbacks?"

His face went pale as chalk. "Okay," he said. "You want to play? We can play." He tapped a few keys on his soft plastic keyboard, bringing up the Company's personnel app, and clicked until he reached her file. Three more clicks revoked her pay-cut. "I don't have final approval on this, but it's in the system. You happy?"

"I'll be happy when it goes through," she said, turning to leave.

"Let's see if you live long enough to collect," he snarled in her wake, and started to say something even worse before she slammed the door on him. She made fists on her way back to the garage, so nobody would notice her shaking hands.

III.

Drivers shared the escort vehicles—except for Maxine's ride, Bad Betty, which none of them dared touch. She had built the beast from the axles up, plating its chassis with hillbilly armor, installing the bulletproof windows, wiring the baby-mini to its swivel-rack on the reinforced roof. On the driver's door she'd painted Rosie the Riveter, modified so that the icon's upraised fist sprouted a defiant middle finger.

"Summarizes my cheery attitude toward life," is how she'd explained that little modification to Corporate.

Tucked behind Betty's wheel, waiting for its systems to come online, Maxine reached into her vest pocket and extracted a cigarette, lit up. Smoking always made her feel better for a few minutes, somehow more capable and together. I'm going to die young and poor, she told Rodrigo once, so who cares how I spend my money?

The garage doors rumbled open, revealing the three trucks idling on the road outside. The sight of vehicles without humans behind the wheel always spooked Maxine, even if half the cars these days seemed computer-driven. Some joker had placed an enormous stuffed bear in the driver's seat of the lead truck, its plump paws gripping the wheel, sightless eyes glittering through the dusty windshield.

119

Maxine gunned Betty into the harsh daylight, the dashboard screen chirping as it communicated with the trucks. Just for giggles, she pulled a sweet, screeching drift in front of the lead vehicle as the convoy's engines revved. Her screen split into multiple views of the road, courtesy of the sticky-cameras plastered on the trucks' bodies: the spider's eye view, she liked to call it.

"What's the load today?" she said. "Fabulous cash and prizes?"

"Like they'd ever tell us," Charlie—not her usual Convoy Monitor, but a good guy—cackled through her earpiece. "Your signal's good. Seventy miles to Albany, next escort vehicle's waiting just off the junction to 87, so, you feeling ready?"

"For all we know, we're risking life and limb to deliver sex toys to rich moms on the Upper West Side." Smoke blasting out her nostrils like dragon steam, Maxine zipped her window down a few inches and ejected the last nub of cigarette. "My drone's up?" she asked. "I don't see its view on my screen."

"No drone," Charlie said, almost too softly to hear.

She slammed a fist on the steering wheel. "Sorry, what?"

"Tony pulled it off, said he needs it somewhere else. I'm sorry."

No drone meant no oversight of the road ahead, and no air support to deal with any bandit in an armored-up. Maxine thumbed the red button on her steering wheel, waking and arming the mini on the roof. Sure, it was a huge violation to prep weapons without a visible threat, lest a twitchy driver draw a lawsuit by accidentally vaporizing a civilian in the oncoming lane—but there were precious few civilians on this blighted stretch of road, and Maxine would rather face outright unemployment than let some hungry punk transform her into a blood-mist.

"I'll talk with Tony when I get back," she said, knowing full well that Corporate monitored these channels. "I'm sure it'll be a productive discussion."

"I have no doubt you'll get your point across," Charlie said, and laughed. He was a cool dude, an ex-Marine who'd served two tours in the Warzone Formerly Known as Dubai and another three in Somalia before a rocket-propelled grenade made a mess of him below the waist. "You want a road report?"

"Please."

"Some jackass pulling circuits in a crap Honda, highway east of Junction Town, shooting deer with an assault rifle. Guess he's too lazy to lie in wait or something. Anyway, not a hostile—to people, that is."

"Any Night Mayor reports?"

"Oh, come on. Really?"

"You come on. Give it to me."

"Two overnight, yeah. But it's crank-heads seeing shadows."

121

"Aw, you're taking the magic out of it. Badass bandit might liven things up."

Betty bounced and shuddered over cracks and potholes, the legacy of a state budget slashed to almost zero after the Last Sequester. The convoy rocketed through the "town" of Meridian (population ten and falling), its once-proud houses now piles of rotten wood and rusty metal, the weedy streets crumbling to dirt. Her grandfather had served as Sheriff here, once upon a time, and the way her father told it, the Old Man had remained the Warrior of Warriors until the day he died of some vicious cancer. *Don't ever roll over for anyone*, her father said the Old Man told him. *Only dogs die on their backs.*

They shot past Meridian, and Maxine exhaled loudly. "You okay?" Charlie asked.

"I hate seeing it like that."

"At least it's not flooded like someplace I could mention."

"Well, that's what they get for building Manhattan on an island." She eyed the dashboard screen in time to catch a flicker behind the convoy—maybe a trick of sunlight and sketchy bandwidth, but maybe a fast follower. Tapping the screen cycled through the cameras, until she had a viewpoint behind the rear truck: a couple kids in a last-century sedan farting smoke, waving crappy semi-autos out the windows.

"You see them?" Charlie asked.

"Yeah, bunch of teenagers." You had to feel sorry for the children raised in this nowhere

122

place, with nothing to do but pop pills and try to jack whatever zoomed past on the road. She had been one of them, a long time ago. "Straightaway next thirty miles, right? I'm raising the truck speed to sixty." She tapped the right buttons on the screen.

"Trucks can't outrun them."

"Oh, I know." Maxine's Work Arm drew her service weapon, which beeped as the embedded chip in the handle talked to the circuits in the limb, which was downloading information from Betty's silicon brain about the relative positions of every car on the road. Buzzing down the front passenger window, she said: "Promise me you won't freak. I can't stand it when you scream in my ear."

"What? I—"

She veered Betty into the oncoming lane and slammed on the brakes, the three trucks barreling past, and as the bandit came alongside her—the driver looked no more than fifteen years old, his neon-green Mohawk bigger than his skull—she extended the pistol and fired four Double-Pop rounds through her open window and into the bandit's front tire, making sure to keep her eyes locked on the target so her brain and nerves and cyber-bits and pistol could all work in symphony to guide home those bullets, which broke into jagged fragments that tore the tire's balding rubber to shreds, sending the bandit fishtailing off the road into the weeds, a crunchy impact she barely heard over the ringing in her ears, and she closed the window again, cocooning in the blessed hum of her engine.

"Target neutralized," she said, and tapped her jaw to switch channels. She knew Rodrigo was waiting, as always, to hear from her.

"Got no drone support," she said, without waiting for him to say hello.

"I know," he said. "That bastard."

"Do me a favor? If I don't make it…"

"I don't want to hear this. You'll make it."

"No, seriously. You get my locker. Divvy it up as you see fit. Sell my Qirui. Use the money to throw a party."

He sighed. "You'll make it."

"Not like I'll have any survivors, anyway."

"I'm sorry."

"Why? It was my bad genes, not yours."

He said nothing, but she could sense his hurt from fifteen miles away. She clenched her jaw— her left eye was twitching, always the first sign of serious upset—and led the convoy through the sweeping turn that marked the beginning of what everyone around here called the Wreckage 500: marshland without civilization for miles, framed by high valley walls that made it hard for a frantic radio call to escape. A perfect place for ambushers, in other words, such as the Night Mayor who'd seemed to dominate the collective consciousness lately—a shadowy figure that Maxine assumed didn't exist, except in the imaginations of a few burned-out escort drivers too superstitious for their own good.

She tapped her jaw again, wanting to apologize. "Rodrigo?"

His reply dissolved instantly to static.

She tapped through her other channels, hearing only a dim crackling, which made no sense: the convoy wasn't nearly far enough into the valley for the radios to die. But a deeper part of her already knew the reason why. Tapping her screen, she ordered the convoy to speed up again. For the first time in what seemed like ages, Maxine felt fear take a double-handful of her guts and squeeze, making her heart speed and breath run ragged. It was almost refreshing, that feeling.

She glanced to her right and saw, beyond the ragged screen of marsh and trees that lined the highway, a dark smudge paralleling her on the access road. Now her earpiece popped and crackled, and she heard the shadow's voice, deep and smooth as a radio host: "Howdy stranger. Sorry to interrupt your call there."

"Back off," she said, swiping her thumb on the touchpad in the middle of the steering wheel, swinging the roof-gun around to underline her point.

"Aw, you don't want to be like that, do you?" her new friend asked. "Can't we be buddies?"

"No." Onscreen, she spied a reddish flicker behind the convoy—probably a second vehicle, because bandits didn't have idiots in Corporate telling them to do more with less. Gee, wouldn't it be great if she had a wingman back there? "You're the one they're calling the Night Mayor, aren't you?"

The shadow snorted. "Cool nickname, huh?"

"Why don't you stop being a coward?" she said. "Come over here." Three seconds with a clear sightline, and her little friend on the roof would cure this man's bad case of jackassery for good.

"Why don't you drive away?" he said, voice bursting with fake cheer. "Go back where you came from. That cargo isn't worth your life."

Maxine could see the rear pursuer creep into the passing lane: an off-roader with two racks of baby rockets bolted to its frame, serious business for all involved. She shifted her eyes right, in time to catch the Night Mayor as he skimmed onto a treeless stretch of access road: a small truck painted matte-black, a spiked plow welded to its fender, brown clouds of smoke farting from its tailpipe.

You really might die, she thought, the fear tightening its grip around her throat. Charlie would call the cavalry once he realized her signal was blocked, but a drone would take too much time to arrive—assuming Tony allowed that to happen.

"You're a good person, I can tell," the Night Mayor said. "I saw you let those kids live earlier."

"Whatever," she said, "I'm not pulling over. And you're running out of time."

He sighed. "Have it your way." An orange flash in the rearview mirror, the off-roader bucking on its back wheels as one of the baby-rocket racks bloomed smoke—she pulled the wheel to the right, taking cover behind the lead truck, but no rocket shrieked past. Instead the sky overhead buzzed white, and her screens snapped black, engine clicking, Betty bleeding speed. Ah yes, an EMP: it was only a matter of time before the road warriors around here borrowed Army tactics.

She hauled the stiffening wheel to the left, inching Betty out of the slowing convoy's path, the trucks stopping five feet from her rear fender. When she tried taking her hands off the wheel, her dead Work Limb refused to unclench—digital rigor mortis. She had to unlatch the limb, glancing in the side-mirror as the off-roader bucked and farted to a halt maybe twenty feet behind her. She accepted its implicit invitation to climb from the vehicle, but not before stuffing her pistol down the back of her waistband, draping her shirt and vest to hide the grip.

Meanwhile the black truck bounced onto the highway in front of Betty, its sides dripping mud from the marsh. Maxine drew a fresh cigarette, torched it, and took a deep drag with tight lungs as the Night Mayor stepped onto the pavement.

He wore an old military coat with brass buttons that flashed in the sun and a tall black hat with a white skull stenciled above the brim. His body was as hard-worn as the clothing, the bearded face rough as a whittled stick. His eyes were the worst, a pair of black holes that swallowed every joule of life around them. It was

127

the face of a man who loved his work, and that work was not kind at all.

"I've never seen you before," she said.

The Night Mayor cocked his head but said nothing.

"Around here, everybody knows each other," she continued. "Cops arresting their nephews, convoy drivers shooting at their brothers trying to rip them off, you know how it goes. Everything's a family affair."

"We're from up north." The Night Mayor nodded over her shoulder to the off-roader, whose passengers hadn't left the vehicle; she glanced behind her and saw their shadows moving behind the dusty windshield. "We heard the taking was sweeter down here." His eyes crawled over her body. "I got to say, that's true."

Maxine rolled her eyes like, are you kidding?

"Whatever: as you said, time's a'wasting." The Night Mayor pointed down the road. "Walk away. We'll give you that. I'm feeling merciful today."

Maxine puffed her cigarette. Another pack would cost twelve bucks, with tax: more than she could afford. She'd always hated living hand-to-mouth, and yet for all the hours she put in, nothing ever changed. Part of that stemmed from her own bad decisions, yes, but it was also the Man, the System, whatever you wanted to call these pricks who spent so much energy trying to keep her in the same hole. Even the bandits were in on it.

"You ever hear of the Murder Market?" she

asked.

"It's that Website, right, people pay to have someone killed?" He arched an eyebrow.

Maxine nodded. "I put a hit on myself yesterday. Created some fake identities, bid a lot of fake cash."

He squinted, intrigued. "Why would you do something like that?"

She took another puff, held the smoke until her chest burned, and blew a perfect ring. "Used it to get hazard pay from my boss."

She thought: I'm sorry, Rodrigo. Our son would have been three. He's the one I would've kept struggling for.

The Night Mayor laughed, his head thrown back. The cigarette flared to the filter, and plucking it loose she flicked it into his left eye—a burst of sparks, the man howling as she snap-drew the pistol from behind her back and pumped three rounds into him dead-center, and before he could hit the pavement she had spun on her heel to empty the rest of the clip at the off-roader, those Double Pop rounds dinging off the bulletproof glass and steel before puncturing at least one thing loaded with gas, because a jet of greasy flame shot from the rear of the vehicle, followed by a sunburst of heat and light, Maxine sensing in that infinite quarter-second that it didn't matter if the oncoming blast cooked her or not— in some small way, she'd just won.

***

©2019 Nick Kolakowski

AN ANTHOLOGY OF NOIR

SWITCHBLADE

ISSUE TEN

TIMOTHY FRIEND
JIM TOWNS
SERENA JAYNE
TIM V. DECKER
CHRISTIAN GOSS
JIM WILSKY
NW BARCUS
GENE BREAZNELL
BEAUMONT RAND
EDDIE MCNAMARA
CW BLACKWELL

POST-BIOLOGICAL-STRESS-DISORDER

Alec Cizak

When Deanna Hanson's consciousness had been uploaded into an artificial body, fifty years earlier, her technician suggested she don a traditional Japanese attitude about the *sameness* that would eventually cocoon her. He'd called it *the comfort of form*. She raked profits from Soy Joy, a pseudo-agra business she'd inherited from her father. She'd watch the bios on the streets below, the unfortunate ones unable to afford immortality, as they clawed and scratched at each other for the five or six miserable decades allotted them. She'd always accepted the trade off—eternal life in exchange for a predictable, daily routine. In recent weeks, or months, she couldn't be certain, she'd felt a change in the signals passing between her artificial brain and her artificial heart.

Melissa Boiler, heir to the Mazacon fortune, turned her on to mooders, psychotronic viruses designed to fool her circuitry into believing she could experience emotions again. She'd popped one and stared at the stark, white walls of her penthouse on Wilshire. The lack of excitement she sensed convinced her the mooder she'd taken had been accurately labeled:

Loneliness.

She tried a libido mooder, inserted the chip in an entry port behind her ear meant for maintenance technicians. Unfamiliar information racing through her cerebral circuits altered her vision. Her pseudo-pulse quickened. She stripped her beige scrubs, thin clothes worn out of a programmed sense of modesty, and flicked her rubber fingers against her rubber clitoris. Observing this in a mirror she hadn't gazed into for several decades, she felt a desire to respond to the absurdity. Laughter, remember laughter? She did. She couldn't engage in it, but she *remembered* it. It spawned no emotions, as her post-biological constitution could manufacture no such inconvenience. Yet, the need to feel something akin to sadness in conjunction with the loss of physical pleasure plagued her. A logic problem, founded on illogical needs.

The next time she spoke with her post-bio peers, she relayed her experience with the libido mooder, called it interesting, but unfulfilling. Lyndsy Camp, who ran a successful cyber-security firm, told Deanna to give a professional bio an opportunity to heat up her circuits. "Seeing how a bio's body works, without the benefits of progress we enjoy?" she said. "Stimulating beyond description."

The post-bios in charge of society had forbidden the use of bios for nostalgic purposes. As with any prohibited vice, this encouraged an underground market. Most bios, in fact, kept their bellies filled with the aid of funds earned through illicit ventures. Deanna Hanson instructed her transport to scoot her down to MacArthur Park where ancient, art-deco buildings disappeared in a constant fog dotted with neon streaks from billboards and storefronts promising nirvana. She ruled out the males. They were notorious for getting rough with post-bios. Status quo opinion attributed their behavior to jealousy—they could not afford immortality and unleashed their anger on those who could. A classic case of the Haves versus the Wanna-Haves. She scanned a huddle of female bios in lingerie, standing outside a business claiming to sell real chocolate. Most of the women's skin betrayed the hideous effects of biological aging. They smeared colors on their

133

faces to mask the tolls of gravity. One woman, however, appeared somewhat unblemished. The pleasant illusion afforded the young. Deanna commanded the transport to roll down the window.

"Air quality is 76 percent undesirable," said the transport's dull, programmed voice.

"I'll take the risk." She poked her head out and attempted to whistle at the young woman. Puckering her rubber lips and blowing air through them produced only a whisper. She said, "Hey, you!" and smacked the side of the transport.

The woman secured the thin strap on her tiny, black purse around her shoulder and slunk over. Her hips moved in a fluid, rhythmic manner Deanna's rigid, manufactured hips could never duplicate. She understood the woman's gait nothing more than a measured display designed to push her product. "Evening, ma'am." The sweet tones of a voice uncorrupted by digital negotiations tickled Deanna's useless belly the way roller coasters had thrilled her as a child.

"Please." She waved off the young woman's manners. "I'm barely older than you."

"Sure." The young woman stared past her. Bored, apparently.

Deanna considered the young woman's behavior an insult. "Are you available?"

"Sure." The young woman's enthusiasm, again, seemingly non-existent.

#

On the ride to her apartment, Deanna learned the young woman's name: Polly. Like a parrot. She asked if she'd been given the name by her parents. The young woman spoke in a voice infected with what the bios called *attitude*. She said, "What's it to you?" Indeed, it mattered not.

134

Deanna had no desire to think of the bio as anything more than a service, a relic designed to distract her from her malaise. A brief, ultimately irrelevant interruption of the comfort of form. Violet scars marred the young woman's legs, something Deanna noticed only because the young woman constantly shifted her position, as though she felt uncomfortable. This seemed absurd, considering she represented a leap backward in evolution. If anything, *Deanna* should have been nervous.

She said, "What sorts of things do you normally do?" She patted Polly's thigh, felt her hard fingers sink into the woman's soft flesh. "And, keep in mind, credit is no object."

"That's swell." The young woman re-crossed her legs, forcing Deanna's hand away. "I got no limits, lady." She ran down a roster of entertainment, all involving, one way or another, her body. "Honestly," she said, "I don't mind licking another woman, but you all…" She stared out the window. "Well," she said, "plastic just doesn't taste so nice." She shrugged. "No offense."

Deanna said, "None taken." She should have had the young woman arrested, teach her to show her betters respect. But her menu of services intrigued her. She said, "I think I'd like to start with something easy for both of us." She then clarified, offering the young woman a credit bump to watch her urinate.

*

Deanna fashioned a toilet from a steel bucket she used to collect rain water when her roof sprung a leak and the building's maintenance bio couldn't fix it in an acceptable amount of time. She watched the young woman unroll her torn stockings and remove her panties. She could not stifle a noise of surprise, prompting the young woman to look between her legs. "Oh yeah," she said. "Most girls shave it, I know. I got better things to do." She untied the burgundy corset suffocating her midsection and breasts. "Besides, keeping it natural keeps the pedos at bay, you know?"

Logic demanded Deanna continue to feign surprise. Hair in unseen places had been deemed primitive even before the wealthy began uploading their minds into artificial bodies. She'd been given the option for a gender-neutral casing when she made the transition. She chose to remain female. None of the models she'd selected from had body hair. She said, "Don't you wish to evolve?"

The young woman stood over the bucket. "Which view you want?" She squatted so she faced her, and then turned around. Deanna focused on the violet marks on the backs of her knees and thighs.

She said, "Drugs?"

The young woman placed her hands on her hips. She pivoted on one foot and said, "What do you think that mooder you popped is?"

The young woman had made an accurate, piercing comparison. "I suppose you're right," said Deanna. "I would like to see your face when you make water."

Unlike the steady ping leaking rain drops produced in the bucket, the young woman's stream, pausing every few seconds, generated a ringing sound, igniting Deanna's memory circuits. She put her clumsy, artificial fingers down the front of her scrubs and touched her artificial vagina and felt...nothing. At least, nothing

136

between the plastic material coating her fingers and the material coating her genitals.

As the young woman wiped between her legs with a towel, Deanna said, "That will be all." The young woman could not look at her as she accepted a bump to her credit and let herself out of the apartment.

She remained seated on the floor, staring at the bucket. She'd asked the young woman to empty it, but the young woman told her it would cost extra. Eventually, she felt an urge to mimic the young woman's ability to make water between her legs. She slipped out of her scrubs and squatted over the bucket. She closed her eyes and pretended to squeeze muscles her manufactured body did not have. She stared at her waving, fractured reflection in the young woman's urine and experienced an irrational weight on her thoughts.

*

Several days passed. Profit trickled in from around the world. Attending to her business, however, failed to distract her from a desire to see Polly again. She took her transport to MacArthur Park and hired her once more. Back in Deanna's penthouse, the young woman set her small purse down and scratched at a particularly nasty violet scar on the inside of her thigh. Deanna had popped several different mooders, including a curiosity virus. She asked, without computing the possible effects her question would have on the young woman, "Exactly what are you using?" Signals crossing her artificial brain sounded an alarm. The bio might take offense, not that the wretched creature had the legal recourses post-bios had; A quick calculation suggested the following utterance might appease the young woman's ego: "I'm not judging you."

Polly reached into her purse and pulled out a string of hard, plastic tubes shaped like lipstick containers. One end round, the other sharp. The substance inside glowed a dark, neon blue. "It's called Neptune." She raised her leg. Her short, Catholic schoolgirl skirt hiked clear of the alluring crease between her thigh and waist. She jabbed the pointed end of the tube into her skin and squeezed. The liquid disappeared. Inside her, presumably. She closed her eyes and stumbled backward. The empty tube dropped from her fingers and rolled across the floor to Deanna. Slumping like an old-fashioned drunkard, the young woman said, "I'll be good in a moment."

"Take your time." Deanna examined the plastic tube. "This is an addictive substance?"

"Wouldn't be killing myself with it every day if it weren't," said the young woman.

Deanna didn't push the issue. She recalled the young woman's analogy—her use of mooders and, what was it called? *Neptune*. How nice to have something in common with the lowly creature. A point of reference, something they could bond over. A *human* connection.

The young woman said, "What'll it be today?"

"Surprise me." Deanna had no idea how she'd produced that response. She wondered how much the mooders affected the technical protocol between her mind and body.

The young woman grasped her head between her hands. Her body shivered and she returned to her normal, coherent self. She nodded at Deanna's crotch. "I noticed you trying to flick one out," she said. "Last time, when I was pissing?"

138

Bios were not allowed to suggest post-biological deficiencies existed. Not *ever*. She could have the young woman sentenced to a reeducation facility long enough to burn her youth and damage her ability to earn credit. Her desire to see more of her demanded she let the offense pass.

"You ever watched a woman orgasm?" said Polly.

She had not. Immortality eliminated the need for procreation. Orgasms, allegedly, were tied to this process. Sometimes. "I understand it's an internal experience."

The young woman shoved her purse to the side. She unbuttoned her white Oxford and freed her breasts from a skin-toned bra. Her asymmetrical areolas made Deanna grin as she thought of her own aligned, identical pink nipples. She reached inside the V-neck of her scrubs and pinched one of them. The synthetic material wheezed. It did not affect her the way it seemed to affect the young woman, who'd laid back and circled her fingers inside her thighs. She brought both hands between her legs and manipulated herself into a series of muscle spasms. As her torso relaxed, sank into the floor, her limbs shook. She calmed and rolled to her side, her skirt still high over her hips.

Deanna said, "Are you okay?"

For the first time, the young woman smiled. Deanna had never seen anything so genuine. "I'm *fantastic*." She licked moisture from her fingers. "I understand why you all pay us as much as you do." The glow vanished from her face and her lips assumed their normal, pouty frown. She adjusted herself in her bra and buttoned up. "I can't imagine how awful it must be, not having a real body."

Good grief. How many more times would she allow the primitive bio to utter such insults? "With all due respect," she said, "my body is more real than yours."

Rifling through her purse, the young woman produced a wad of chewing gum, bit off a chunk, and ground it in her mouth like a mindless cow. She pulled her panties over her legs and stood, allowing her skirt to fall into place. "Sure thing." She asked for her credits.

Deanna's protocol regulators insisted she hold to the topic, demand an apology. She said so. The young woman said, "It's no big deal."

"No," said Deanna. "You've suggested your regressive flesh is superior. That's simply impossible. *I* am progress. *You* are the past."

"Fine, fine." The young woman's eyes walked the ceiling. "I'm scum, you're an angel. Can I have my credits?"

Deanna decided she'd received the closest thing to a mea culpa the young woman could offer. "All right, then." She bumped the young woman's credit. Before the young woman left, Deanna said, "I hope this momentary discomfort won't prevent you from returning, should I desire your company again."

"No sweat." The young woman showed herself out of the apartment, leaving a trace of her perfume in the air, a disruption in Deanna's nasal sensors she could not decipher as anything other than a curious change in the atmosphere.

*

In the young woman's absence, Deanna overdosed on mooders, attempting to recreate the feelings generated by her presence. She

140

mixed them—libido, curiosity, jubilance—and caused multiple shorts throughout her artificial brain and synthetic limbs. Her mind and body shut down and an alarm alerted Cedars-Sinai to send technicians to her penthouse. Once they'd cleared her system of the mooders' viral programming, they plugged her in to a charger and brought her back to life. She'd been unaware of the damage she'd caused, had no memory of shorting out. "Did I die?" she asked.

The female of the two bios sent to operate on her said, "In a way, yes." She'd colored her hair pink and allowed tattoo artists to draw cartoons of skulls and demons on her arms.

"I paid for immortality," said Deanna.

The woman's coworker, a rather unhandsome bio with a receding hairline, said, "You can't put these viruses in your system. You'll void your service agreement." One of his eyes opened and closed so fast Deanna almost didn't notice. "We won't mark it on your file," he said. "Just stop using mooders."

"They don't outlaw those," said the female, "you cyborgs might disappear." She clasped her hand over her mouth. "I apologize." Calling a post-bio the c word could doom a bio to a life-sentence reeducation facility.

Exhausted signals from Deanna's artificial brain suggested she let it go. She said, "Watch your tongue in the future."

Long after the technicians left her apartment, she sat at one of three windows in her penthouse overlooking the city. Transports competed on Wilshire, nagging bios in crosswalks to "get a move on," whatever that meant. She'd allowed the technicians from Cedars to dispose of her remaining mooders in the disintegrator in her kitchen. She imagined having the lithe body of a bio, of being able to shrink herself and dive after them. Her brain dismissed this as something called a fantasy, something her logic circuits rendered pointless.

*

As time flattened once more to the comfort of form, to a predictable wheel upon which she watched the obscured sun rise and fall over the hazy horizon as she sat at a compact interface and monitored the ebb and flow of her corporation's profits, foreign thoughts intruded. No, not thoughts. *Emotions.* Irrational declarations:

I want to see Polly.
It would be nice to see Polly again.
I need to see Polly.

The yearn reminded her of her youth, when she'd still been human, regressive, and required sustenance three times a day. If she went without, pain swelled in her belly. Panic set in, and the belief she would perish if she did not stuff the remnants of a dead animal down her throat dominated her attention. This urge to spend time with the professional bio struck her as no different. Logic, however, protested:

This makes no sense at all.

To which her minority circuits said, *I will die if I do not see her again.*

You cannot die, logic responded.

To which her scant, fledgling emotions said, *Death can mean many things.*

As her brain negotiated this most illogical claim, her body stood on its own and exited her apartment. She ordered the elevator to take her to the ground floor. On the street, she signaled for her transport and instructed it to drive her to

MacArthur Park. She hired Polly once more, barely able to simulate breathing the moment the bio sat next to her. The young woman didn't speak much. Mostly, she pointed to several neon signs and expressed fascination at how they glowed in the fog. Such a simple creature. And yet, Deanna couldn't stop electricity from seasoning her mind and limbs when she looked at her. Any time she focused on the young woman's soft skin, the perfect curve of her neck, the lines formed by her chin, her delicate jaw, her artificial heart beat faster, harder. She touched the young woman's cheek, expected her body to burst and spill a tidal wave of fluids. Her rubbery fingers dented the young woman's flesh. Polly's face turned red. She pulled away from Deanna's caress. "We need to discuss business."

What the young woman had in mind, in fact, involved watching an old movie on a video screen Deanna rarely used. "You have access to the outlawed archives?" said the young woman. "Let's watch a chick flick." Deanna asked her to clarify. "It's porn for the superior half of the species," said Polly. She cycled through a menu of ancient Hollywood propaganda on the screen and said, "Oh, this one will do it." She chose a movie called *The Notebook*. The young woman travelled a buffet of emotions as the story progressed. She laughed, she grabbed her mouth and made noises suggesting she'd been punched in the belly. At the film's conclusion, she wept. Her tears streaked her makeup. She wiped her face with the sleeve of her thin, flower-patterned dress and looked at Deanna. "Don't you get it?"

Deanna decided she would bring the young woman in off the streets permanently. She could

143

save her from Neptune, as the technicians had saved her from the mooders. Against all protests from her artificial brain, she said, "Polly, I love you." And once she said it, even her logic circuits calmed. Yes, it made sense. She'd been alone for decades. She did not enjoy it. This young woman would change that, keep her company during the hours her corporation required no attention.

The young woman giggled. "I'm sorry," she said. "I didn't mean to, you know…" She coughed and cleared her throat. "I'm flattered. I've never had a cyborg say anything like that to me. But I could never feel anything real for you." Her head tilted to a forty-five-degree angle. She adopted a condescending glare. Like this changed her position in society. Like she had *any* business looking down on a post-bio.

Deanna pointed at the door to her apartment. "You don't want to spend time in a reeducation facility, I suggest you get out of my sight. Forever."

Waving an open palm as she stood, the bio said, "You still owe me."

"You're a *prostitute*," said Deanna. "You want me to call the authorities?" Oh, she would show her. She would show her *exactly* who ruled the world.

The young woman strung her purse across her shoulder and left.

An immeasurable hollow developed in Deanna's synthetic gut. As though a cannonball had charged straight through the center of her body. She knew she should produce water, the way the young woman had, from her eyes. She knew she should keel over and sob in uncontrollable heaves. But she hadn't been designed for such a gauche, primitive display. And so, she remained still. For hours. She did what she could to block the horrid picture of traveling the expanse of infinity, remembering this moment, forever unable to do the one thing necessary to quell this illogical pain. Somewhere along the map to eternity, she promised herself, her interest in profits would obscure the weight of this injury. The comfort of form, a comfort she should never have abandoned, would return. Just a matter of time, a commodity she would learn, once more, to cherish.

***

©2019 Alec Cizak

GALATEA IN THE
GARDEN OF EDEN

Matthew X. Gomez

"I hear you are an individual who can find people."

Tremblay didn't bother looking up from the display projected on the scarred particle board table in front of him, scrolling through his email and news feeds, face bathed by the soft cyan light. "I'm not a pimp."

"I am not looking for a joy girl. Or boy. I'm looking for a specific individual."

Tremblay looked up. The person standing in front of him stood out like a violet blooming in a concrete lot. The clothes—dress shirt, jacket, and suit pants all in dark charcoal—alone cost more than his rent for a year, and an expensive watch glittered on their wrist. Hair was shaved close to the skull, cheek bones sharp enough to part silk, and a bit of tasteful make-up. They could have been male or female or neither, not that it made much difference to Tremblay. Half-rim glasses with a mirror sheen obscured their eyes.

He looked at T'Anna. She slouched by the bar and gave him a shrug, using two fingers to point out two men standing awkwardly in the bar Tremblay used as an office. They shifted in their polished shoes, unsightly bulges under their jackets. Could be drugs or could be guns. Probably guns.

"All right." Tremblay switched off his display. "What's money like you looking for?"

The suit pulled a phone from their pocket, swiped across to a file. Pressing a button, a video played on the table. Blonde woman, young, no more than twenty. Maybe twenty-two. Fresh faced, but her eyes looked haunted. She kept glancing over her shoulder at whoever was taking the video, her mouth twisted down into a frown.

147

Hard lines around the eyes, drawing her brow down.

"She is missing," the suit said. "We think she is in the Barrens. We made inquiries. More than one source suggested you as someone who would be able to find her."

Tremblay felt the corner of his mouth twitch into the semblance of a smile. "Why'd she run?"

The suit paused. Tremblay wondered if his question was being relayed back to its handler through a hidden earpiece, if what he talked to wasn't more than a puppet, the strings held by an unseen master. Could be the suit had a radio drilled right into its head.

"Who said she ran?" the suit asked.

Tremblay's smile faded, replaced by an all too familiar frown. "She did," he said, pointing at the video. He shook his head. "It doesn't matter, much. What's her name?"

"Does it matter?"

Tremblay worked his tongue over his teeth. "Yeah, it might. Or at least, if you know what she might be calling herself. People around here change names like clothes."

"Nicole Grayson."

Tremblay rolled the name around in his head, but it didn't mean anything to him. "All right. Something like this, it will cost you five thousand." The quoted number was fifty percent more than his usual, mainly because history taught him that people with money usually had no idea what it was actually worth, and partly to see if whoever was behind the suit would bite.

"That is acceptable."

Tremblay bit back a curse and nodded instead. "It isn't much to go on, but I'll see what I can pick up. How can I contact you?"

"You do not require a portion of the fee up front?"

Tremblay's frown deepened. "A quarter up front. Non-refundable. I find her in a state less than what you showed me, I still get paid, is that clear? You're paying me to find her, not make promises I can't otherwise keep."

The suit paused. Tremblay figured whoever was on the other end of the connection was slowly masticating that bit of information. Rolling it around in their mouth. Wondering if it was too bitter to swallow.

"That is not our preference, but we understand." It offered its hand to shake. Tremblay stared at it as if he'd been offered a week-dead fish, but eventually he reached across, touched his fingertips to the cold, rubber-like skin. Fucking synthetic. Looked human. Tried to act it, but it was a computer dressed up to look human. Corporate types liked to use them as go-betweens. If a synth caught a bullet, it was expensive to replace but it meant the suits didn't have to worry about the potential of dying. They often ran autonomous software, but Tremblay heard some corporate types were able to remote pilot them, get their hands dirty without ever having to leave their office. Some of them were getting better at acting human, but it was still just that - an act.

"Call us at this number when you have information for us." It passed a flat black card across the table. The only thing on it was a number embossed in silver.

After a transfer of funds, the synth exited along with its bodyguards, and Tremblay allowed himself a sigh of relief. His back and underarms felt soaked through.

"Got a job?" T'anna pulled up a chair, spun it around and straddled it. Neon designs danced on the shaved sides of her head, but her eyes were a warm brown Tremblay could fall into for hours. Not that he was T'anna's type: tall and muscular who weren't all that interested in talking.

"Yeah. Need to find a little lost rich girl."

T'Anna frowned. "Is that it?"

Tremblay shrugged. "Maybe? I doubt it. Nobody with any sense comes running into the Barrens."

"Yeah, unless…"

"Unless they really want to get lost, I know."

"So what are you going to do?"

Tremblay raised an eyebrow at T'Anna. "Are you asking because you are curious or because you want a piece?"

She smiled, but the way she did it made it seem more like she was baring her teeth getting ready to strike. "Figured you could use the help."

Tremblay frowned. "You smelled money."

T'Anna nodded. "Yeah. But I'd also hate to see anything happen to you. You're all right, Tremblay. You pay on time. You don't take liberties. You treat me like a person. Goes a long way."

He snorted. "All right, I'll keep you on retainer. If there's any additional windfall on this, you get cut in at twenty-five, all right?"

"Yeah, all right."

"Good. Now go away. I've got calls to make."

*

Two hours later, Tremblay and T'Anna stood outside a tenement building, a squat concrete turd of a structure. The street lights had long burned out, and the only sign of security cameras were the exposed wiring where they'd been

150

pulled out. Overhead, the ever present whirr of drones echoed down to the streets, but there was more than enough buildup overhead that they weren't much of a concern.

"Place is a shit hole, Tremblay."

Staring up at the boarded up windows, the doors covered in yellow police tape, Tremblay couldn't help but agree. Trash littered the street in front of the entrance, and the only sign of life slouched at the corner.

The boy, face pocked and scarred, one eyelid drooping more than the other, limped over to them. "Looking to score?"

Tremblay shook his head. "No. Wait, hold on. We're looking for someone."

The boy smiled, showing gaps where teeth should have been. The rest were black and rotten, broken stones in a mouth of ruin. "I know lots of someones."

Tremblay pulled out his phone, swiped over to the video. "Her name's Nicole. Might be going by Nikki, or something like that. I heard a guy named Freddy might know where she is. You've seen either of them?"

"She's pretty."

"Yeah."

The boy shook his head, his brow furrowed. "Pretty things don't last long around here. Freddy's inside though. He knows lots of things."

"Thanks."

"Can, can I have the video?"

"Got a phone?"

The boy fished a battered phone, the screen long cracked, the edges looking gnawed on, from out of a pocket. Tremblay tapped his phone to the boy's and the video copied over.

"Thanks."

Tremblay smiled, but it came off as tired and worn. He'd seen the sores on the boy's arm, saw the way his hand twitched. If he lived longer than three months it would be a miracle, and down in the dark and the grime miracles didn't happen.

The door into the tenement stood open and unlocked. No one living there had any belongings they didn't keep on themselves. Tremblay breathed shallowly through his mouth and T'Anna made a slight gagging noise at the stench of rotting garbage and human waste. Someone piled garbage against the walls, and things shifted through the piles disconcertingly. Two people, heavily wrapped in layers of clothes and with gas masks firmly affixed stood flanking the one closed door in the lobby.

"We're looking for Freddy," Tremblay said.

The two guards looked at each other, some unspoken communication conveyed via the smoked glass lenses of the masks. The one on the right knocked on the door and waved them on, but then the one on the left put out an arm, barring T'Anna's entry. She reached into her jacket, and the guards tensed, but Tremblay waved her down.

"It's all right," he said.

"Are you sure?" she asked, eyes fixed on the two guards, her hand still in her jacket. "We can get the answers some other way."

Tremblay smiled. "I'll be fine. Wait here, okay?"

"And if you don't come out?"

"Give me an hour. I'm still not out, have fun."

A wide grin split T'Annna's face and she looked at the two guards with hungry eyes.

The guards opened the door and Tremblay entered. The air smelled cleaner in the room. Still slightly stale, the result of recyclers having to work overtime, but still. The lack of garbage definitely helped. Freddy sat by himself, stretched out on a couch, some movie projected on the discolored and cracked wall in front of him. He glanced over, shifting his bulk, small eyes narrowed through thick goggles.

"I know you, yeah? Yeah. Tremblay, right? Mister Finder-Man."

"Yeah, that's me."

"So what are you looking for Finder-Man? A good time? A good girl? A good boy? Some pills? Patches? What?"

"I'm looking for a girl. A friend of a friend told me you were the man to talk to."

Freddy laughed and he pointed a single fat finger at Tremblay. "See, see, I know. Everyone looking for the same kinds of things. But if it's you that's asking, must not be just any joy girl you are looking for, eh? Looking for something special. Exotic." Freddy chewed that word out, like he practiced it in the mirror for hours to make sure he pronounced all the syllables distinctly.

Tremblay reached into his pocket for his phone.

"Easy, easy," Freddy said. Tremblay wasn't sure when the gun appeared in Freddy's hand, but there was no denying it was there now, looking small in his ham-sized hand, but the black abyss of the barrel no less intimidating.

"Just getting my phone out."

Freddy grinned. "Better be all it is."

Tremblay removed his phone, flicked his thumb over to the video still of Nicole. He passed it over to Freddy.

"Yeah, maybe I've seen her. Girl like that, she sticks out down here."

153

"Okay, so where can I find her?"

Freddy put the gun down on his leg. "You want me to tell you for free? Get fucked."

Tremblay sighed, reached into his pocket. Freddy raised one caterpillar thick eyebrow, but didn't go for his gun. Out of his pocket, Tremblay produced a small white pill bottle. "Purple haze," he said. "Good dreams, little side effects. Sell them by the dose you'll get a good return."

"Someone must want this girl bad," Freddy said, reaching out for the bottle.

"Where first," Tremblay said, holding the bottle just out of Freddy's reach. "And steer me wrong and we'll have trouble."

Freddy grinned. "If this how you always do business, no trouble at all. You'll find her at Garden of Eden. Calling herself Galatea. And Mister Finder-Man?"

"Yeah?"

"Come talk to me again if you're alive at the end of this. Maybe we can do business. Proper like." Freddy turned back to the movie.

"Yeah."

*

"The fucking Garden of Eden?" T'anna grimaced when Tremblay told her where they were going next. "I'm not sure you're getting paid enough for this shit."

"You want to bail?"

"No I do not want to fucking bail, but..." she raised her arms up to the sky, showing off the scar tissue where the grafts had been placed. Sure it had been a few years, but scars took a long time to fade, even when properly treated. "This whole thing seems like it's getting more complicated."

Tremblay snorted. "Yeah. Welcome to my life. But if it was simple then the people running that synth wouldn't hire people like me. Either it's outside their neatly ordered lives or it's dirty enough that they don't want to touch it themselves. So they get people like me to do the dredging."

"And you hire people like me because?" T'anna asked, her tone light.

"Because sometimes people don't like the questions I ask, and I'm a lousy fighter."

They headed down a nondescript alley, its most telling features being the lack of graffiti and a working security camera. Tremblay walked up to a unmarked door and rapped on it. He could hear the whirr of a camera lens focusing on him, then the door clicked open.

Upon entering, the first thing he noticed was the smoke… not the usual smog of the city, but a heady mix of illicit chemicals permeating the air. Tremblay felt a dull, thudding bass beat reverberating in his chest and he caught half-whispered conversations through the thick woven hangings separating rooms instead of doors. Three men sat in the entryway, all alike in the way they wore their handguns strapped under their arms, and the way they wore one side of their hair long to the shoulder while the other side was shaved close to the skull. They all had the physiques of men who trained to fight, lean muscle and sharp reflexes.

"You lost?" one of them asked. He wore a close trimmed beard and crimson glasses, images dancing on the lenses.

Tremblay shook his head. "Looking for someone in particular. Calls herself Galatea."

"What about her?" the one on the left asked, pointing at T'Anna. His skin was flaking and peeling, like he'd spent too much time getting rained on, the acid stripping off the skin. "She looks like she can move."

T'anna laughed. "Yeah, I can move, but only on my own time."

"The girl?" Tremblay held up his phone with her picture.

"Yeah, she's here. You got to pay to go in though."

"How much?" Tremblay asked.

The man with peeling skin quoted a number. Tremblay frowned, but transferred the amount over.

"Don't damage the merchandise, you hear?" the man with the glasses said.

"Yeah."

He pushed through curtains, nearly tripping on a prone form half-buried in the pillows covering the floor. He placed his feet with care, not wanting to step on anyone. He followed the sound of the music, eyes scanning the debauchery. He felt the bile in his throat rise. More than one of the rooms featured people dancing, people fucking, people ingesting all sort of substances. None of them fit Nicole's description, all of them looking hard-used and close to burn out. He pushed past a heavy curtain, and saw her. Not as she was in the picture, frozen and perfect, but swaying, sweating, eyes staring far away to a place that was anywhere but where she was right now. Instead of the blouse and slacks of the picture, here it wasn't anything but a lace bra and a thong, sweat flowing down her limbs as she grinded to the beat thudding from the speakers.

156

There were other people in the room, but none of them paid any attention to her.

"Huh. Nice tits," T'Anna said. "What? She does!" she added, when Tremblay gave her a side eye.

He approached her, his hands up, palms out. "Nicole?"

Her eyes snapped into focus and she froze, a small rodent trying to avoid a predator's gaze. "Who are you?"

"My name's Tremblay. Some people are looking—"

Her eyes snapped into focus and she collapsed against the wall. "No, no, nononononono."

"Easy, easy." He knelt down as she twisted her head back and forth. "I'm not going to hurt you."

She looked at him through splayed fingers. "Then why are you here?"

"Someone asked me to find you, that's it."

"Then what? Tell them where I am? Hold me until they get here? And if they hurt me… what, your conscience is clear because it wasn't your boot on my face?"

Tremblay frowned and shrugged. He looked around the room, at the people slumped on the ground, most barely hanging on to awareness. "You're better off here?"

"Not the point," Nicole groaned. She pulled up a blanket from the floor, wrapped it around her body. "Did they tell you why I ran?"

"Not my problem."

"What's she here for?" Nicole asked, jutting her chin out at T'Anna. "In case I get out of line?"

T'Anna sniffed, but Tremblay shook his head. "This isn't exactly the nicest part of town. It helps to have someone watching your back."

Nicole sniffed. "Yeah? I wouldn't know what that's like."

"You want out of here?"

Nicole nodded. "I thought I'd be safe here. Thought I could hide." She let out a laugh that was closer to a sob. "I… I didn't know…"

"You've got clothes?"

"They are around her someplace."

"Find them. Find someone elses'. We're leaving in five minutes."

T'anna stared hard at Tremblay.

"What?"

"Are we still going to get paid?"

Tremblay thrust his hands into the pockets of his coat. He felt the hard plastic of the stun gun he kept there. "You'll still get paid."

"Yeah? Because twenty five percent of nothing is nothing, you understand? I'm not interested in nothing." T'anna's fingers twitched and a long thin blade glinted in the half light of the drug den.

Tremblay frowned. "Did I stutter? You'll get paid, even if it means I'm dipping into my own pocket. You said you trusted me, remember? Don't tell me you're losing faith already."

Nicole found clothes somewhere, a baggy shirt and a skirt that didn't quite match that fell to her knees. Old boots rounded out the look.

"Come on," Tremblay said.

"Hey, where do you think you're going?"

Tremblay looked up, saw one of the men from the front room, the one with the acid peeled skin. Tremblay palmed the stun gun in his pocket.

"Heading out. This is my cousin. My aunt told me to find her."

"Huh. I don't care if she's your sister, you're not leaving with her," he said, pointing at Nicole. His other hand held a blocky plastic gun. Looked like the kind someone might knock off in a backroom with a second hand 3D printer, the kind that would either spit bullets or blow up in your hand. Maybe both. Probably both.

"Yeah, why's that?" Tremblay asked.

"Hands out of your pockets, all right? They better be empty."

"All right. You didn't answer my question though. Why can't we leave?"

The man with the gun looked at Tremblay. "You can leave. She can't. She owes, man. She pays in cash or she pays in trade."

"How much?"

"Fift--"

The man with the gun never got to finish his thought. The whole time he'd been talking, T'Anna had been sliding forward, shifting her feet a bit at a time. With his focus set on Tremblay, he didn't see her moving, the silver line of the blade in her hand slicing his wrist. He dropped the gun, fumbled for it with his off hand. He opened his mouth to shout, but her knife entered the side of his neck, and she twisted and wrenched. He dropped with a gurgle, blood spurting from the wound. He clutched at it with his hands, eyes bulging, feet kicking against the ground. The other people in the room, blissed out on the chemical of their choosing, paid no mind to the person rapidly becoming a corpse.

"Is there another way out of here?" Tremblay asked.

"Huhhhhh…." Nicole's eyes focused, found the body of the man. She turned, retching into the corner.

"I'll take that as a no."

"Hey, Vic, what's taking so long? You better not be manhandling the merchandise--" One of the other guards entered the area, parting the curtains with his hands. Tremblay pulled the stun gun from his pocket, sent an electrically charged dart into the man's neck. The guard fell, twitching, to the ground.

"Let's go!" he barked, grabbing Nicole by the arm and pushing her ahead of him.

The guard with the glasses looked up, his eyes coming into focus. Tremblay hit him with the stun gun as he was fumbling with his gun, and T'Anna kicked him in the ribs until she heard a wet crack. Outside, a long black sedan was parked. The two bodyguards stood at attention, arms folded over barrel-chests, eyes unreadable behind dark shades. One of them opened the door to the sedan, and the synth stepped out onto the sidewalk. Nicole made a noise like a trapped animal, her entire body tensed to run. T'anna grabbed her arm, held her firm.

"Our thanks, Tremblay, for tracking down Ms. Grayson."

Tremblay narrowed his eyes. "What are you doing here?"

"We've been following you. The card had a transmitter embedded in it. We will take her now."

"Funny thing is, I don't think she wanted to be found… at least not by you."

"What she wants is immaterial. Property doesn't get to have an opinion."

Tremblay narrowed his eyes, saw the bodyguards tense. T'Anna was behind him, out of eyesight.

"You fuck…" Tremblay spun as the man with the glasses stumbled out of the Garden of Eden, one of the plastic printed guns in his hand. The other guard followed right behind, a collapsible baton extended. The bodyguards drew their own guns, flat black hunks of metal with abyssal barrels.

"Down," Tremblay shouted, pulling T'anna and Nicole to the ground with him

The plastic gun didn't explode in the man's hand, and a bullet caught one of the bodyguards high up in the shoulder. Whatever the gun was loaded with, Tremblay doubted it was standard ammunition given how the bodyguard's back exploded outward. He fell back as the other bodyguard pulled the trigger. He missed Glasses, his bullets stitching along the baton's chest and stomach. Tremblay fired his stun gun, the dart hitting high in the bodyguard's thigh. He twitched, falling over, continued to shake and dance from the current even when Glasses took off the top of his head with another shot. Glasses aimed the gun wildly, swerving between Tremblay and the synth before settling on Tremblay. His lips pulled back from his teeth, but he'd lost track of T'Anna. She rose up behind him, a grim spectre of death. She wrapped one arm around his arm, forcing his gun down. He grabbed her other wrist, tried to force her hand away from his chest as she pressed the knife ever closer. She sank her teeth into his neck and he howled. He lost his grip and the knife sank into his chest.

The synth stood there, its expression unreadable on its inhuman face. "You have made

161

a mistake, Tremblay. We know where to find you. We know who you associate with. You can still turn this around."

Tremblay pried the pistol from the bodyguard's hand.

"Hey, T'anna."

"Yeah, boss."

"How much are synth parts going for these days?"

T'Anna grinned through the bloody smear of her mouth.

"That's what I thought."

The gun bucked in his hand.

*

"Don't you want to know why they were after me?" Nicole asked. They sat at the bar, Tremblay having slid an envelope toward her. A solid chunk of his cut from the sale of the synth and the car went to what was in there, but T'Anna was happy and there was something to be said for that.

"You've got a new identity, plane ticket to São Paulo, and some walking around money," Tremblay said.

T'anna sat in her usual spot, some fruity drink in her hand as she shared a laugh with a local joygirl. She raised her glass in a salute to Tremblay. She didn't seem worried about the shitstorm he might have called down on their heads.

"That doesn't answer my question," Nicole said. "You could have—"

Tremblay raised a hand. "Stop, okay? Yeah, could have done a lot of things. Could have had T'Anna there drop you at Garden of Eden. Could have called the synth and told him we found you, but it was on him to get you out. Could have walked away once we got you out. Don't ruin this

162

by asking why, and don't make me regret what I did, okay? You get a second chance. Not many people in this life get that. So don't ruin it by asking a lot of unnecessary questions."

"You're a good man." She leaned over, kissed his cheek, then collected her envelope. A local that owed Tremblay a favor waited outside to drive her to the airport. Tremblay watched her leave then turned back to the bartender.

"Another?"

"Yeah. To second chances."

Tremblay could only hope that whoever was running the synth would forget about this. Looked like he'd be paying T'Anna extra for the foreseeable future to have an extra set of eyes watching his back.

***

©2019 Matthew X. Gomez

163

TORNA NAILS, MINDBENDER

James Edward O'Brien

They threw the infiltrator in headfirst. She'd cold cocked a leatherneck. Left an MP for dead.

They tore off her hood. The locker stank of rotten produce. Standing water. The only thing she could make out was an IR monocle that hovered before her in the darkness.

Someone jabbed a barrel in her spine. It was still hot.

A disembodied voice: "What brings you off-moon?"

"Nails, Torna. Specialist, first class."

"She's got her shtick down pat," he conceded, administering a swift backhand.

A second voice rose behind her. A woman this time. "Specialist, first class? Cripes, Sarge, even terrorists are handing out stripes nowadays."

The sergeant twisted the band on Torna's eye patch until it snapped. Cool air hit her socket. "You born ugly or you lose that eye in a scrap?"

"Nails, Torna. Specialist, first class." She repeated it like a broken record—a mantra.

The soldier behind her administered a sharp gun-butt to her spine. Pins-and-needles blossomed down her legs. "You don't start cooperating and you'll be shy your other eye, too," she warned her.

"Nails, Torna. Specialist, first class," Torna reiterated. She choked back blood from the fractured nose they'd given her. "Mindbender Cadre."

"Cripes, Sarge, she's a mindbender!"

"Grease her!" barked the sergeant.

White-hot backfire from the soldier's DEW lit up the room. The gun's pterodactyl whine reverberated deafeningly off the reinforced walls.

'Like shooting fish in a barrel,' thought the corporal. Only she'd been sealed up inside with the fish. She was drowning, tasked with shooting her way out. All the Kevlar and dragon scale in the multiverse could not stop a mindbender.

The sergeant fumbled for a light switch. There was a whiff of ozone. The buzz of neon. He scrabbled for the blade in his boot as his corporal discharged her DEW at the walls.

The sergeant lunged for the mindbender. His knife whistled passed her, but there were only so many ways the mindbender could evade him in this sweatbox. He threw the brunt of his weight against her.

His ratchet knife found her windpipe, and the shrill cacophony of gunfire and screams died as quickly as it has risen. The mindbender went heavy in his arms.

Killing was seldom this personal. He knelt before his victim and clutched his stomach. It was all that he could do to not evacuate his bowels right then and there.

"Vemen," he cried, "Vemen?"

He prodded the corpse—his corporal's. Air gurgling out where he'd opened her throat. It had all been a mindbender's trick.

166

Through the shock, he could feel the prisoner needling around in his head; he could almost feel the eyes of his corporal staring back up at him. And then his mind froze. It did not go black or still; it did not offer solace or refuge from the morbid misstep he'd made. The mindbender had him locked down in his own head. Regret, remorse, and sororicide made hostile cellmates.

The mindbender kicked out the door and dragged the sergeant outside. A communion ship was waiting; its hatch agape like some verdigris beluga chiseled from stone and cast iron.

*

Airman Goddaughter did not like mindbenders. They made an art of shirking the stringent protocols and doctrines that, in his mind, served as the bread-and-butter of the modern military hierarchy. Every mindbender Goddaughter worked with dwelled in a moldy gray area somewhere *between* the bread and the butter. Mindbenders, after all, existed somewhere between what *is*, and what *seems to be*. Specialist Nails liked to prod him and claim there is *only* what seems to be, but he wasn't buying what she's selling.

She was not in the mood for taking cheap shots tonight, though—Nails had taken too many shots of her own. She sat quietly, listening to the lodestones grind in the belly of the communion ship as it repelled them out beyond the pull of the Petrichor Moon.

The captive sergeant-inquisitor cupped his head in his hands and bawled like a baby. Goddaughter turned in his cathedra to survey their captive.

"Caught a real live one," he acknowledged, chomping on an unlit stogie. "He gonna be like this the whole ride home—or you just working your voodoo on him?"

Specialist Nails frowned, directing Goddaughter's gaze back toward the starry porthole in front of them. "Keep your eyes on the road, Airman."

"Buckle up, Specialist," he shot back at her.

Nails eased into the passenger's cathedra and forced the captive into the seat beside her. Prehensile straps unfurled from she and Goddaughter's chairs, crisscrossing their chests and constricting.

Nails motioned toward the sergeant-inquisitor. "His belt's wonky. Can't have him free-range."

Goddaughter let slip a wicked smile. "Can't we?"

The airman dropped the communion ship into a nosedive. With he and Nails strapped down, the sergeant-inquisitor became the sole ratty sock in the spin cycle. The captive cursed and caterwauled. Nails slouched down in her cathedra to dodge the violent tilt-awhirl of limbs tossed around like doll parts.

"Enough," Nails ordered. "There's gotta be something in the Petrichor Convention prohibiting this sort of thing."

"Nosedives?"

"Don't play dumb, Airman," she warned him.

"Ma'am, yes, ma'am," he conceded.

He brought the ship up so abruptly Specialist Nails felt like she'd left her lunch in her jackboots. The sergeant-inquisitor hit the back wall like a fly against a windshield.

"You'd think a flyboy so hung up on protocol would adhere to the articles of the Convention that apply to detainee treatment."

'She'll never get it,' thought Goddaughter.

In his mind, every rule and regulation served as a barometer for how much you can get away with—how far you can *bend* the rules without breaking them. Mindbenders have no blasted barometer. In Goddaughter's mind, they were loose canons 24/7, except when it suited them not to be.

At the same time, the symbiotic relationship airmen shared with their communion ships frightened Nails. All of her people had distinctive gifts, but the precision with which an airman could pilot these pet rocks was uncanny. Propelled by lodestones that worked against the moons' polarities, airmen controlled the when and where of each voyage telekinetically.

Nails was no novice when it came to noodling around *inside* peoples' gourds, but airmen had the ability to trigger phenomena in the corporeal world—at least where their ships were concerned. It was like their clunkers were an extension of themselves, no different than a monkey's tail or a second skin. It was part of them, and they were part of it. Specialist Nails was never quite sure where one ended or where the other began.

*

The journey left the captive with a dislocated shoulder. The cellar where they'd tossed him boasted a soda machine and recliner with macramé cushions—more shrink's office than pokey. The mindbender entered with a second woman: wiry framed, piercing copper eyes, her hands clad in thick, metallic gauntlets. She had one of those faces. She sized up the captive.

"That's him," she confirmed. She limped toward the captive. "Remember me?" she asked him, unsmiling.

The sergeant-inquisitor glared at her cockeyed. "Maybe. Maybe not. Can't tell you crater-hoppers apart half the time."

The woman wriggled out of her gauntlets and slapped her right hand on the table before him. Her trigger finger was severed at the knuckle.

"Jog your memory any?"

His eyes lit up, like an artist surveying his magnum opus. "My work, yes." His nonchalance flustered her.

Specialist Nails had to hold herself back. She wanted to get in his head, put things in there that he'd never come back from. Nails just bit her lip. "Ensign Peko?" she began.

Her CO cut her off. "I want Goddaughter down here. Between the two of you, I want to know who exactly is at fault for the condition of this hostage."

Hostage. That verbal clarification of his title sent a flush of prickly heat through the sergeant-inquisitor's face. He squirmed a little in the recliner.

Nails threw Peko a palsied salute. She dashed off to sniff out Goddaughter. The ensign locked eyes with the hostage.

'This woman looks so sad, playing at soldier,' thought the sergeant-inquisitor. He'd grown accustomed to working in palettes of anger, anguish, fear, *terror* even—but sadness, sadness was alien to him. Sadness, in his mind, was the byproduct of certain empathy he lacked—a quiet, illusive beauty that titillated his sadist's heart.

He looked into eyes as cold as his own. For the life of him, he couldn't remember her. There had been so many. But those eyes...this one was a masterpiece. He'd left nothing left there.

Anger flared in the ensign's throat. "The regs down here have a nickname for you. The Petrichor Persuader."

The sergeant-inquisitor could not mask a smug smile. Peko shot him a gnarled backhand.

"Cute." Peko struggled to retain some composure. "But anyone who's suffered at your hands knows there's no moniker that can soften, that can humanize, what it is that you do."

"I serve my people. My nation."

"You serve your compulsions," she spat. "Your nation was lost once special interests caught wind of the fact that the atrocities you yourselves once suffered through—the purges, the Marifran Farhud—atrocities you'd once pledged to fight in all their forms—simply lay dormant in the worst of all of our natures. A junkyard dog they could rouse with a stick and use for their own ends."

The sergeant-inquisitor dabbed his split lip with his tongue. "You think you're gonna bait me with political rhetoric?" He cackled. "Bring me into the fold like one of those limp-wristed greenhorns, so fresh off their mamas' teats that they don't understand how the world goes round? You of all people; you know exactly who you're *talking* to. Save your breath," he griped, "take a finger. It's all the mercy I ever showed you."

There was a gentle rapping at the door. Nails poked her head in.

"You've found him?" asked Peko.

Nails nodded. "Aye, Ensign."

"Inside. The both of you."

*

Ensign Peko tore into Goddaughter. "Article Six of the Petrichor Proclamation expressly prohibits endangering the physical well being of a subdued captive."

A grin crept across the sergeant-inquisitor's face. He saw right through Peko—she as much a hypocrite as the rest of them. The sergeant-inquisitor rubbed his swollen jaw where minutes before the ensign had cracked him.

"My pet rock got ornery on reentry," conceded Goddaughter. "She oft needs more coaxing than piloting, truth be told, Ensign. She's a cold shrew, that one—doesn't just wrap them cockpit tentacles around any old soul."

"Yet you and Specialist Nails appear to have come through the void unscathed," noted Peko.

Goddaughter brushed some lint off his crimson anorak. "Appears so, ma'am."

"Well," she warned him, "I can't court-martial a sentient piece of space flotsam, can I?"

"No, I'd imagine that would be damn near impossible, ma'am," he concurred.

"So if we have any repeats of this sort of thing, Airman, you and you alone will be held fully accountable."

"Yes, ma'am," he saluted.

"Dis-missed," crowed the Ensign, "Specialist Nails and I have work to do."

She plucked a cigar from Goddaughter's anorak pocket as he made for the door. Peko kicked out two metal folding chairs collapsed against the wall. She dragged them across the linoleum with lumbering intention; the hoarse screech of the runners was spine tingling. She propped them up right in front of the hostage's recliner.

She beckoned toward Nails to sit. "You're not off the hook," she warned her, "Goddaughter's a glorified taxi driver when all's said and done, Specialist. If something had happened to this sonuvabitch in transit, it'd be your neck."

173

"Kid gloves," smirked the Petrichor Persuader.

"Shut up," snarled Ensign Peko. She turned to Nails. "Just be more careful next time."

Nails offered no excuses. She didn't need to. Mindbenders were such a rare commodity that they only faced reprimand when they screwed the pooch beyond repair: cases of sudden death or damaged armaments.

Peko fired her stogie. She crossed her legs and read the list of his crimes from her green steno screen.

"Kidnapping."

"Lawful detainment," he corrected her.

"Torture." The ensign's voice cracked a little.

"Coercion," he shrugged.

"Mutilation," she retorted. Nails could see what digits remained on Peko's right hand trembling ever so slightly.

"Body modification." He said it with a jack-o'-lantern grin.

The ensign leapt from her seat. Nails sensed the satisfaction on the hostage's face. Ensign Peko snatched up her flimsy folding chair and raised it, poised to strike. Specialist Nails did not flinch. Nor did the hostage.

"Hit me," he bated her.

Nails stepped between captive and captor. "And fail where they've failed?" she cautioned her superior.

"Failed?" crowed the sergeant-inquisitor. "We butcher you wholesale."

174

Nails cocked an eyebrow. She could not disagree. "Adherents to the same genocidal tactics that were used to nearly snuff your own kind off the maps. A failed experiment if there ever was one."

'This one has sad eyes too,' he thought to himself, 'I could snuff out that glean in an instant.'

Peko lowered her chair. Her chest heaved. Specialist Nails needled her way into the prisoner's gourd. All that hate left his thoughts brittle, scattered—an apocalyptic game of pickup sticks.

"The boot feels much better on the other foot, doesn't it? You want to kill me," said Nails. "The ensign too."

"Don't take it personal," the hostage sniggered. He glared at the ensign. "Should've killed you right the first time.

"I *see* you," warned Nails. "I can look right through the shattered lens through which you see the world. How much you hate it all. Everything. The uniform just gives you a means to channel it. I *see* that it's not me, that it's not just the ensign. The whole world is your punching bag."

He spat at her from across the table. "Crawl back into your crater—and get the hell out of my head while you're at it."

A silence fell over the room, a stalemate that hung for what felt like forever, until Ensign Peko uttered one simple word: "Why?"

"Why?" he snarled. "Why'd a hopper board that rig last month with a neutron detonator strapped to her chest? Why'd a mindbender smuggle his way onto the Leisure Ship Largo and prompt half the crew to swan dive out the airlock?"

"We're a people with few options at our disposal," the ensign responded. She wiggled the nub of her missing finger. "You think we have a battalion of legislators and lobbyists laying in wait at the reservation?"

"All you animals know is violence." He reared up in the recliner.

"Are they handing out legal degrees and diplomatic solicitations for tilling soil or working hydraulic rigs now?" asked Peko. "Without any clout, without the funds to buy the ears and attention of any lunar representatives, violence has become our solitary voice."

"I got news for you," he snickered. "You're losing. We got ships. We got bombs. We got the weight of the Lunar Trifecta behind us. What the hell is it that you've got?"

"The same as anyone else," lamented Specialist Nails. "Only what we can reap with the tools we've been given. The same as you."

"You're nothing like us." The disdain in his voice was palatable.

"You're right—the violence you commit is sanctioned."

"Because you're terrorists."

"Because the trifecta sees there's profit in your brand of destruction—arms contracts, resource extraction—whereas ours carries a heavier price tag. Just a crapload of starving children and questions that beg answering."

"Read your histories," he challenged her. "A gaggle of citizen militia playing war seldom comes out on the winning end of these sorts of scenarios."

There was an ice-cold matter-of-factness to his delivery, a detachment that made Nails want to throttle him into oblivion. Ensign Peko was less reserved. She kicked aside the table and had her fists locked on his collar quick as a crater cat.

Nails was afraid she might kill him, afraid her CO was becoming unhinged. The ensign felt a prickly effervescence blossom in her head. She knew Nails was digging around in there.

She could *feel* Nails taming her synapses as if they were an unruly team of sled dogs. Blasted mindbenders. *It was against protocol*. But so was the laundry list of pains she wanted to inflict upon their captive right now—as if his death might somehow compensate for the countless shallow graves pocking Petrichor, or possibly wash clean every bloodied inquisition room floor so that she could forget the last seven years. So that she could be at peace. She'd killed her way to knowing better a long time ago. She loosened her vice grip on his collar.

"Article six of the Petrichor Proc—" he began to remind her.

"Nails," said Ensign Peko, "he's all yours."

*

177

The sergeant-inquisitor crossed his arms. "So here we go again," he said.

He rocked back and forth, making the recliner coils squeak. Specialist Nails did not like being alone with him, even though there were guards posted within earshot, even though the hostage was a slight man who she could break in a thousand different ways. It wasn't what *was* there that frightened her, though, but what was not: the incredible absence in those eyes.

Mind-bending hostages who proved tough nuts to crack was par the course, but she'd never learned to sit easily with the ones who were empty inside once she'd cracked them wide open.

"The tables have sure as hell turned, haven't they?" he muttered.

"No," Nails corrected him. "They haven't. It's the same old enemies across the same flimsy table locked in the same old song-and-dance."

Having the sergeant-inquisitor at her mercy provided Nails cold comfort. She knew they could toss him, torture him, and torch him to little effect outside of incurring the wrath of the lumbering, corporate oligarchy of which he was just a pawn––like shooting a mad dog when the owner was the one who needed putting down.

She moseyed toward the vending machine. Jabbed at a button. The machine spit out a can. She opened it. Toasted him. "To the same song-and-dance, for time immemorial."

"Time immemorial." His eyes did not meet hers.

She pushed the can across the table. "Drink?"

He eyed her suspiciously. He examined the can. He waved it under his nose before taking a slug. He could already feel her riling up the fury hive in his brain.

"Let's go for a ride," she beckoned.

*

The dying sun turned the world outside the color of a timeworn photograph. The rarebit had already gone cold.

Hands cracked and bloody from an age steeped in scalding dishwater. Teats. Weary knees.

'Not the guise of a sergeant-inquisitor,' he frowned. 'The children should be back by now.'

They'd gone down to the settlement guardhouse to pester soldiers for credits and candies. He didn't like them down there—some of the older kids had a penchant for rowdiness. The teenagers. The ones who'd lost parents at the onset of the war. The ones who were now of an age where all that dead weight began to slacken their steps, anchoring them to a land and a life dispossessed of joy and imagination.

It was no place for children. There had been incidents. Kids throwing rocks. Orphans selling unspeakable favors to uniformed killers for scraps to eat. The moon had always been a cold, unforgiving place, but it never truly felt that way until these killers came from Petrichor with their ships and decrees and bloodshed. There'd been

179

an eruption down the quarry. Screams. Canon fire.

'Long past the time that the children first left,' he told himself. 'How much of the afternoon would an impatient child be willing to kill begging for sweets and pocket change?'

He plotted the whipping he'd give them for being late for dinner. 'They're not bad children,' he fretted, 'I'd spare the rod to see them safe home. But to worry their mother so, a child must learn the weight of repercussions.'

The colors outside began to dull as the sun crept behind the mountains of the moon. The street outside was empty. No footfalls. No laughter.

A watched pot never boils. He tried to distract himself with an article about the migratory habits of lemmings, but he couldn't stay focused—eyes drawn to the picture window and a street with no children, a sky with a sinking sun. He began making deals with a god he'd neither believed in nor had time for, as any good mother in dire straits would.

'Just let them be safe and I'll cherish them as the ungrateful buggers would be hard-pressed to appreciate,' he fretted. "As they deserve."

His eyes volleyed between the words on the steno screen and the window. The sky had gone so dark it was no longer worth looking. He scrabbled toward the door and flipped on the porch light. His middle boy had sprained his ankle—nearly flayed his knee to the bone tripping home blind one night.

'All those scars and growing pains—map legends of danger and chance—it's a wonder any of us make it through unscathed,' he thought, trying to force a chuckle. But no laughter would come.

Stomach in knots and heart aflutter, he bartered with his shrewd, deaf deity: 'Please, god, please, spare the children...my children.'

LED lights from an approaching police cruiser painted the kitchen walls cobalt and crimson. All he could do was hold his breath and hope they would pass for another house. Another mother's bad news.

There came a rapping at the door. This is where Specialist Nails held him still: in a mother's horror of unknowing. In-between breaths, somewhere between grieving and dreaming.

But he was no mother. The sergeant-inquisitor's mind was no more fertile than the shriveled womb of the old sow whose memories the mindbender had tried to use to haunt him. She'd just as soon trigger a supernova with a penlight battery.

"Ensign," she called weakly through the door.

Peko entered. She and Nails exchanged not a word. Nails shot her a nod—a timid glance.

"I told you," Peko scolded her. The ensign slapped her DEW on the table and killed the safety. "Sometimes, a mad dog needs putting down—despite the right or wrong of it. There is such a thing as being beyond redemption."

"Are you sure?" sneered the sergeant-inquisitor.

The mindbender's psychic push forced his hand to raise the gun to his temple. She looked right at him. His last great work: another one broken. He'd left nothing but fear in her eyes. He could almost smell it on her.

Death came calling sooner or later; that did not fluster him. As white-hot plasma opened the side of his head what mattered to him, in that fractured mind splayed in chunks across the walls of that bunker, was that he'd won.

***

©2019 James Edward O'Brien

sundown

Rob D. Smith

The War was more fun, thought Manny as he dodged the looping left hook of the drunk kid. He should let the asshole connect. Watch his expression as he cracked his knuckles on his polymer laced bones. But the dilettante's father was the client. And Manny was the bodyguard. A BCD discharged soldier didn't have a lot of options. Legal options that was.

Manny had jumped at the chance for some action instead of guarding another NuBoy's underground hydroponic farm. K.C. Prime was full of them now. The rush to add Green and sustainable food sources within the city proper had been a concession of the War. And the winners were proceeding full speed with their Green Initiative.

Manny stayed out of politics except for when he was a fighting pawn. He got kicked out before he aged out of the military when there were few survivors from the prairie frontline. His enhancements were as old school as him. Today's soldiers were land, air and sea drones. Any foot soldiers were vatted in a lab and brought to rapid physical maturity.

Maybe this son of a bit-coin wrangler was born a week ago. Maybe he was a yipping poodle the rich bastard bio-hacked into his offspring. Either way Manny's patience had run its course.

"Kid, stop. Its my job to keep you from hurting yourself."

Kirk Alklander flexed his muscles. But it was genetics and a stim bed body. He was a hothouse orchid not a ragweed that had been tested out in the cracks of plastcrete and sun. All show and no go.

"That's right Manny. So, get my goddam drink you fucking tin soldier."

184

"Tin..?"

"Yeah that's what my dad calls you behind your back. You like it?"

Manny just seemed to shimmer a second then flicked a short kick into Kirk's shin. The kid howled in pain. Manny put his thumb in Kirk's mouth, his fingers around his jaw bone and pulled the kid too him.

"You're leaving here with a broken tibia and if I apply more pressure a mandible dislocation. Are we done?"

The kid tried to nod but Manny had a solid hold on his lower jaw. He mumbled yes with a mouthful of thumb.

Manny let go. "I think I'll go get that drink now."

The kid let Manny get across the crowded dance floor before he started cursing him. His tactical enhancements applied to his ambient hearing as well. He could filter out the deafening explosive gunfire from the soft footsteps of an assassin in battle. Now his brain felt like it was white water rafting down the Yellow River. The bartender smiled at him.

"You riding shotgun on the Alklander brat?"

"I was. Now I'm out of a gig." And like that Manny realized he would have to hustle up something else. He couldn't use the Veteran's Hospital for treatment. Dr. Tsung only took favors and hard physical currency for his back alley medical practice.

She went under the bar and came up with an amber bottle. "You've earned a free pour from the special stock. Reserved only for bartenders after hour bitch sessions."

185

She poured him two fingers into a rock glass with a hunk of ice. He saluted her and took a healthy pull on the drink. Oak and smoky.

"Pappy?"

She grinned as she slipped it back under the bar. "Yeah and that's all you get for slapping around Alklander."

"Hades, I'll go ace him right now if it gets me more bourbon."

"Not tonight cowboy."

"Why not tonight?" A tall woman in the most expensive business suit Manny had ever seen joined him at the bar.

"Private stock madam. I'll be glad to pour you anything else." The bartender pointed to the well-stocked wall of alcohol behind her.

"I'll pay double for the private stock." She smiled like a jungle cat.

The bartender pulled the bottle back out and poured two fingers and dropped another chunk of ice in. She went to hide the bottle of bourbon back under the bar but the woman held up her hand.

"Double for the whole bottle."

The bartender tilted her head and put the bottle back on the bar. She held onto the neck until the stranger waved her iWristlet under the bar credit scanner.

"Manny Villager. Come with me." The tall woman headed to an empty VIP section of the club.

Manny got his drink, shrugged at the bartender and followed her. Whatever this well-heeled lady wanted at least he could drink some fine bourbon while he listened to her bullshit.

He sat across from her on an opulent synth-leather couch. She had unbuttoned her suit coat and looked at ease.

"I would like to hire you for a security job."

"Who are you?"

She leaned forward. "I notice you don't wear any wristlets or goggles. Do your tactical optics still work?"

This lady knew way too much. "Mostly."

She touched her iWristlet again and flicked two fingers off the surface of it towards him. Information popped up on his optic interface display. Text and images overlayed on his vision. It was some lab facility on a campus near midtown.

Manny blinked the display away and asked her forcefully again, "Who are you?"

"Laverna Duran. It's not who I am but what I am. I'm the lead director of Talos Security Services."

Manny frowned. "I can't work legit security gigs anymore. But you know that. Unless you need a burnout military vet to do some black bag op?"

She dramatized taking a swig of her bourbon. "I have an opportunity for you. Nothing lethal but skirting legalities a bit. The information I sent to your tactical neuro is a company I'm doing business with. I designed their security system."

"You aren't just the face of Talos?"

"I could give you my veritas Mr. Villager but let's say it's long and capable."

Manny saluted Laverna and eased back into the chair. He was sitting with a puppet master. He should just relax and wait for his string to be yanked.

187

"Yes, this is off the screens because even with my resources I could not get your record expunged for any security services. I need you to test the security system I have installed at Herod BioFuel Institute."

"That's it. Just break into their facility? Debug your system and protocols."

"I want you to try and steal the 13C Bacterium Key-drive from the facility. The place cannot be hacked. Even if the Key-drive is removed off property it is always stored in a Faraday Case that cannot be opened by usual or unusual means without destroying the contents. So even offsite it's secrets cannot be uploaded to the Cloud. It's hack proof. Hardware to hardware interlock release."

"Is the bacteria key weapon grade stuff?"

"Bacterium. This is not for military applications. It's potentially the most lucrative sustainable biofuel source today."

Manny slapped his thighs. "Everything has military applications ma'am. Do I get paid an outrageous sum for stealing this bacterium key and exposing your security flaws?"

"Enough to help pay for a proper medical clinic treatment. Do you wish to accept?"

"Sounds like the proverbial cakewalk."

She turned off her mega watt smile. "Do not treat this like a smash and grab at the local bodega Mr. Villager. The danger is real. Law enforcement and my security team will know nothing except you are a hostile threat. Your brain could end up even more scrambled."

"Easy sis. I know what you want. You've tested it against the elite already. You just want to see if some enhanced troglodyte like me can circumnavigate your pristine world."

"I've seen the scalpel. I need to see the mace."

Manny poured himself a full glass of Pappy. The filters in his kidney and liver diluted the effects of alcohol. "I want half up front. And expenses for equipment and resources."

"The money is already in your account Mr. Villager."

*

Manny was tucked tight inside the Peregrine Class Drones belly compartment. The drone circled a figure eight pattern at 10,000 ft altitude above K.C Prime. His recon of the Herod BioFuel Institute proved that he would never be able to physically breach it without triggering alarms or being caught. A hired hacker would only get him so far through the physical barriers and access protocols. Talos Security Services at Femme Duran's helm created an impregnable defense.

Manny had to flush the 13C Bacterium Key out. Disrupt all the security features at the facility enough to make them move the target to somewhere more secure. Manny hired one man capable of handling his hacking and drone needs. He smiled as he thought of the expense account, he would hand Femme Duran.

The equipment was in place. All systems were green.

"Piglet. Initiate Operation Honeypot."

"Copy that Tigger. And I must say that these callsigns are *bhenchod*."

"When you're footing the bill, you can make the names Piglet. Now send in the Rhino."

Manny watched on his optical interface the live feed from the CCTV feed outside the Lab. The audio picked up a high-pitched keening sound. Then a blur crunched through the

189

southwest retaining wall. The Rhino was a Type II Ground Drone. A breaching implement that could carry human or munition payloads. No soldiers in it this time. DIY gelatin napalm jettisoned from the drone's chamber. A keystroke from Piglet and the gelatin ignited. A fire not impossible to extinguish but close.

Piglet aka Ansh Banerjee earned every credit Manny spent. The kid was an intuitive drone jockey. *Kid?* Ansh was in his late thirties now. He worked mostly freelance for environmental contracts these days. Manny knew he didn't need the money. Ansh needed the Action.

The Rhino breached 30 meters into the facility. A loud klaxon wailed. The active fire suppression system kicked on but the chemical fire raged. The security guards approached warily and any facility scientists and crew evacuated the building.

"Wave two Piglet."

"Aye aye Tigger."

Manny patched into an interior hall camera on the northeast side of the facility just in time to see a coalescing black cloud rush through. The hum of the Hive class swarm drones was like a dirt bike engine. He followed their wake and caught up to them on another camera attacking the security team with high voltage stings.

"Tigger. They are moving the Honeypot. Copy, they are moving the Honeypot."

"Copy that."

Manny pulled his optical feed back to the Peregrine drone. The drone camera could see as well as a real falcon but with infrared and other enhancements. An armored Talos flight transport zoomed off the ground and circled west. Ansh directed the drone to follow from above matching their speed.

"First responders and law dogs all converging on the facility. The Honeypot has not picked up any escorts. We are free to engage."

Manny triple checked his belts and rigging. "Start my descent on mark one. Three, two-"

"What the fuck soldier!" A female voice broke in on their comm.

"Who is this?" Ansh sounded nervous. Probably wondered how someone could access his secure line. But someone of her skills could.

"This is our benefactor Piglet. She should know better than to interrupt an ongoing op though."

"I'm paying you for thievery not demolition Vil-"

Manny interrupted, "No names on the comm. Call signs only. I'm Tigger. He's Piglet."

"And you're now Eeyore ma'am," said Ansh.

"Why don't I just end our arrangement this moment and hand you over to the authorities?"

Manny said, "You could. Then I could destroy the target. I don't think your clients would retain you after that. And it might be tough to find new work after this leaked in the civilian network."

"Or?" she asked.

"Let us finish the op. I return your product safely. You smooth things over with the police and your client. Then I'm paid for all my hard work showing the weaknesses in your defense."

The comm ran silent for only a few seconds but it seemed forever. Manny hoped he had played the right card. Hitting her need for wealth and power.

"Continue your operation. I'll send the meet coordinates when you have the target. And we will discuss the rest of your payment."

Manny touched his forearm keypad sheath. He entered a code and pressed send. "No. I'm going to need you to send the full credit now. I'm sensing your trepidation. I'm uplinking the full bill of services to your CloudDrop account."

He heard Ansh suck air. Then the comm was eternally silent again. She broke back.

"You won't be able to spell trepidation after I crack your damaged skull some more. You aren't worth this much." The rage tore through the channel.

"Fine. Piglet I'm going to jettison on mark five. On mark one, send the Peregrine into the Talos transport at maximum acceleration."

"Copy Tigger."

Manny counted down. "Ten, nine, eight, seven-"

"Fucking jarheads. Stop. Payment was sent."

Manny checked his account. "Smart play Eeyore. Now don't take this personally but Piglet switch to Umbra Channel Zulu Twelve."

"Copy Umbra Channel Zulu twelve."

Laverna said, "Don't show up without-"

Manny cut her off. "Send me the meet coordinates shortly. Tigger out."

*

On Zulu Twelve, Ansh jabbered, "*Mader chod*! you can't do that with our money. My money."

"Did you just call me a eunuch again?" He felt his pulse throb in his temple.

192

"I siphoned credits from my savings *gaandu*!"

"Now I remember that one is asshole." Manny pulled up his tactical overlays but they flickered. He banged his helmeted head against the interior wall. The visuals steadied.

"Piglet line me up so I can go get the Honeypot. Drop in Mark one."

Ansh grumbled some more curses on the channel but the drone's visuals lined up with Manny's war brain. Over K.C. Prime the clouds were patterned as randomly as man could create. Outside the walls the cloud cover dissipated. Burned away by the omnipresent sun's angry eye. The transport flew over the Wall away from cover.

"Mark three, two, one." Even with all his modifications and enhancements, Manny felt the tug of gees as the peregrine drone dove to its prey. The armored transport vehicle went from a pinprick on his optical screen to a bowling ball in two seconds. In ten seconds, he would be on top of the vehicle. He braced for impact.

The drone pulled up at the transport cutting descent velocity in an instant. Manny's breath barked out. He watched on his optical screen as the drone latched to the transport with its magnetic talons.

"Everything's pristine. I'm going for the Honeypot." The bay doors opened. Stale wind rushed in. Small silica particles tikking against hard surfaces.

"Don't fall *gaandu*. I need my money."

"Don't worry Tigger's bounce." Manny unfolded a large rectangular modular frame. He placed that frame against the top of the transports roof where it adhered tightly. He next plugged in a cable to one corner. At the other end of the cable was a hand held trigger. Manny pumped the trigger three times and the frames phosphorus filament ignited burning a rectangular ring on the roof.

Manny pulled a small flashbang grenade from his vest. He kicked in the roof cut and tossed the grenade in. Boom, pop and some residual smoke streamed out of the opening by the high-altitude winds. Manny made sure his cable rigging was still tethered to the drone then dropped through the hole.

One Talos guard was holding his head in his hands trying to regain his senses. Manny pulled his XM-25 9mm pistol and shot a hornet round into the guard's center mass. As the guard shivered and fell to the floor from the electrical charge, Manny slid to the side of the van and checked for other threats.

The only other guard piloted the vehicle. Behind a locked clear ballistics proof door. Looks like Plexi-glass but stouter than reinforced steel. Manny could hear him rattling on his comm.

"Lima One is breached! My partner is down. We need assistance ASAP! Repeat ASAP!"

Manny tapped on the glass. "No one can hear you son. Your comm is shaded. Now open up like a good lad."

The guard pulled his handgun from his shoulder rigging. "I'll cut you down."

Manny saw his expression. This guard was a bulldog but just a pup. He might bite him a little but he only had baby teeth. Baby teeth were still sharp though.

"Piglet take control of the transport and set her down."

194

"Roger Tigger."

Ansh's drone was close enough to hack control of the transport to his computer. The offensive KRACKware worked even better when the wireless signals were in physical contact.

The guard grabbed at his steering yoke and used all his strength to change the descent. He called out, "Lima One needs help. Repeat Lima One needs help."

"You can put that on a loop kid. But no one can hear it. We have everything locked down. Enjoy the ride, don't mess with me and you'll live to guard again."

Manny held onto the grab rail along the ceiling of the transport. He kept his 9mm pistol in his other hand. Behind the glass, the guard had his weapon pointed at Manny. Amped to engage.

"I said relax. You can't open the door and-"

The guard stamped on a floor pedal and the glass door slid open. He fired three taps into Manny's chest. Manny rolled backwards with the impact and came into a shooting stance. He shot the guard on his chin. The ceramic round splattered conductive gel all over his face. 25,0000 volts turned off the guard's lights.

Manny took some zip cuffs and lashed both guard's legs and wrists together. "Damn Piglet! I thought you had control."

"I got it. I got it. Not like you haven't been shot before sir."

Manny checked his tactical armor. The nano-plating had only taken some frag marks. The military built good shit even if it was fifteen years old. The new armor systems were lighter, tougher and harvested energy from the soldier's kinetic movement. *Lord he wished they hadn't kicked him out of the marines*.

195

"You got eyes on the Honeypot, Tigger?"

Manny shook away his revelry and went to the rugged alloy Faraday Case secured to the wall. He didn't have the biometrics to open the locking system. And he didn't possess the fine tools to force it open it without destroying the contents. He could only trust Laverna that the Bacterium Key-drive was inside.

The transport came to a stop on the ground. Manny climbed back out of the hole in the roof. The sun so bright even the shadows under the drone were well lit. His helmet visor darkened adjusting to the brightness. He put the briefcase in an interior compartment and got into the drone's jump seat. He synched up with the drone's computer and sealed the bay door.

"Did she send the drop coordinates?" His headache returned.

"Coordinates are a go. Just south of here. A few klicks."

"Copy that. Take us to the drop Piglet." Manny took deep cleansing breaths to clear his head.

The peregrine drone soared off over the bright scrub grass plains.

*

The drone flew past the colossal wind farms that helped power K.C. Prime. The vertical axis turbines twirled in the searing breeze sending kinetic energy into the gearbox at their base then routed to the city. Solar energy, bioenergy and other renewable sources kept the lights on. Multicorps like DynaTran were trying to be the new lords of capitalism by harnessing these alternate fuels.

Clean energy for the Green Party and their constituents. But the hands that made it were still dirty. Still fought over by soldiers like him. War was another sustainable source of energy. Ballistic energy.

A building showed up on the drone's crisp hi-def visuals. It filtered out the harsh UV rays from the sun. Citizens didn't have to live behind the gargantuan Wall of the city proper but living out in the Big Dry took resources. Outlanders were either wealthy or kooks.

This residence looked of money. The architecture designed with a slanted roof made from concrete, stucco, plas-steel and filtered glass. Only one upper floor. It likely had a basement structure. If Manny had to venture, he believed this to be a Talos Security Services property. Maybe through a shell owner.

"This is the place Tigger. I didn't pick up any heat signatures. Looks clear."

Manny unhooked from the rigging and rolled out a side door on the drone. His visor immediately frosted up from the sun light. The exterior plated body armor reflected heat waves from his body. The tactical suit reacted to environmental ranges whether a sweltering rain forest or the sub-zero artic.

"Keep your bird in the sky but not too high. Watch for non-friendlies."

"Copy that. Now go get my money Tigger."

Manny reached back in the compartment and took out the metallic Faraday Case. He walked towards the house as the drone rose from the ground. Dirt and silica whipped up in the engines wash.

"Our money Piglet."

Above the front door an obtrusive security camera spied on him. That must have driven the architect insane. When Manny reached the door, the locks clicked open. He kicked dust off his boots and went inside.

An open floor plan connected the kitchen, dining and living room. It was all very sterile with modern furniture pieces and art work. There was the occasional reclaimed wooden table to warm up the place. Still Manny would take this 4,000 square foot lifeless space over his coffin size flat back in the city.

He held up the Honeypot. "Come out Laverna. I have your precious cargo."

She spoke over the house smart speakers. "One moment. Tied up with something. Just set the case on the table and have a seat."

Manny put the case on the horror of a coffee table. He decided to stand. He subvocalized to Ansh to check the sitrep.

"Still pristine," said Ansh on their clandestine frequency.

Manny pulled his pistol. Something was off. "Laverna get out here or I'm blowing a hole in this case."

Her voice came softly over the sound system. "Go ahead and shoot it. Do what you're good at and make a mess."

Manny backstepped towards the front door. "Play your mind games with someone else. I have my creds. I delivered like I said I would. We're done."

"Sorry Manny I'm way on the northern side of K.C. Prime. Collecting the actual 13C Bacterium Key. Thank you for drawing all the attention to the decoy transport."

Manny was almost to the door. "Bullshit! You're close by."

"In that atrocious house? Now I've only seen images but does it smell pretentious too?"

Manny subvocalized again to Ansh. "Piglet are we still green?"

"Yeah Tigger. Still clear."

Laverna's voice cut through their shadow channel. "How about now? Are you still 'green'?"

Ansh sputtered, "How did...oh *mader chod*! Tigger get out. Lot's of spinners on the way. Look like cops."

The alloy Faraday Case on the table popped three times and landed on the oriental rug. Smoke ringlets escaped from the briefcases seam.

Manny sprinted to the front door but it wouldn't open. The locks were back on.

"Unh Unh sugar. I need you there for your shoot out with the police."

He spun looking for a side window. The entry way would be fortified but an interior window might not have as much reinforcing. He hoisted a heavy chair up and slung it at a glass window. It just bounced off.

"I picked this place special. You've heard of Panic Rooms? This is a Panic House. Impenetrable. Or in your case inescapable."

Manny said, "Piglet, I need a hole on the northwest corner of this shithole. Think you can make that happen?"

Ansh responded, "New door coming up sir. Take cover."

"Oh, sweet boys that isn't going to happen."

Manny heard a keening sound getting closer.

"I don't have control. Stop...!" said Ansh.

Krakoom!

199

Manny felt the impact close. He ran to the wide opened windows that faced the snowcapless mountain range. The drone sunk half its broken fuselage into the dirt. A wing was missing.

"What happened Piglet?"

No response. Maybe comms was down." Piglet come in. Copy?

"Piglet can maybe drool but he won't every copy again. The synapse spiral feedback was too much for his little mind to handle.

Ansh! "If he's dead, I'll rip your head off."

"Lucky for me I'm on my way to the Pacific Coast territory."

Manny roamed the interior looking for an exit point. "Who do you really work for? WestCal Dynamics? Or the PacCo Gov?"

"You should have asked those questions before you took the job? See you've gained something more valuable than creds. You have wisdom now."

Manny went to the garage. A boxy antique 4X4 Land Rover was inside. Petrol engine. No wireless for fake Laverna to grab onto. He opened the vehicles door and looked inside. The keys were in the ignition.

"You think that fossil is your salvation? It doesn't have the power to bust out."

Manny rushed to the reinforced garage door. He checked the hinges and structural weak points. Then he hung what concussive grenades he had left and pulled their triggers. He had three seconds to rush behind the SUV. The upper two exploded at the same time followed abruptly by the lower placed grenades.

A lot of smoke billowed. He swept the smoke away to check his handiwork. Four solid scorch spots where the phosphorous charges burned. He hoped that it was enough.

"This is why you got kicked out of the marines. You don't know when to quit. Well that and your neural network was leaking into your brain pan. Couldn't be trusted in the field."

He got in the Land Rover and turned the key. The engine rumbled on. Manny hadn't used a key to start a vehicle in ages. The exhaust emitted petrol vapor flowering the garage with environmentally harmful particles. Only rich people could afford this decadence.

"How's the head Manny? Hallucinating yet?"

"Keep yammering bitch. I'll be seeing you soon."

"I see now why you took this op. Or any of the high-risk jobs. You want to go out fighting. Not laying in a hospital bed. Don't worry. When the police get here, I'll let you reach your destiny. To die with guns a blazing."

Manny pressed on the petrol pedal feeding the engine. It growled and he knew the evil bitch hadn't popped the hood and checked. This fossil had big teeth.

"Check my discharge papers again lady. It'll tell you what I told the marines. I leave when I'm damn good and ready. And I'm ready."

Manny gunned the SUV and crashed into the bay door. It gave a little. He shifted into reverse and rapidly backed up as far as he could banging into the back wall. He kicked the pedal hard and the Land Rover cannoned into the door. It buckled and he was through.

He turned the vehicle around to the front driveway as fast as he could control it. The west end of the drive blocked by three cop spinners.

201

He thought about hitting the scrub plains but he had a third a tank of fuel. The eternally angry sun set behind the cops. The orb had a twin brother that winked at Manny then disappeared.

"You didn't make any difference jarhead."

"I got out on my own. That's all I needed." He saw more police spinners hovering to his north and south. Corralling him.

"I won't go to prison."

"I never thought you would."

Manny floored the Land Rover at the spinner blockade. The cops targeted their assault weapons at the approaching juggernaut. Manny drove straight into the setting sun.

***

©2019 Rob D. Smith

AB NEGATIVE

FOURTH ACT ENTERTAINMENT PRESENTS A FILM BY TONY PANA "AB NEGATIVE" ANTHONY REESE TONY PANA MARGAUX COLARUSSO
RENAUD LECUYER AS THE COUNT ADRIAN RALLO MYZ AND GIO TROTTA PRODUCED BY TONY PANA AND ANTHONY REESE
EXECUTIVE PRODUCERS TONY PANA AND ANTHONY REESE ASSOCIATE PRODUCER TRISTAN BAILEY CO-PRODUCERS MATHIEU TROTTA
PASCALE ELOY STUNT COORDINATOR ANTHONY REESE GIO TROTTA DIRECTOR OF PHOTOGRAPHY JASON MACCA THIBAU D1
MUSIC RALLO MYZ SOUND STEPHANE MARCILLE SOUND MIXING ALEXANDRE DELEGLISE
STORY TONY PANA ANTHONY REESE AND STEPHANE MARCILLE WRITTEN AND DIRECTED BY TONY PANA

ORIGINAL POSTER BY QUENTIN COLICE

SWITCHBLADE
Outlaw Apparel
LOS ANGELES
EST. 2017
WWW.SWITCHBLADEMERCH.
COM

"The Creature from the Black Lagoon with The Seven Year Itch"

• Author and editor **James Reasoner** delves into his short novels for *Mike Shayne* written as **Brett Halliday**; his PIs Cody, Delaney, and Markham; his Redemption series, his Wind River series with **L.J. Washburn**; and much more.

• **Ward Smith** remembers Armed Services Editions—digests that are not digests.

• **Peter Enfantino** tackles *Startling Mystery Stories* No. 1–18, and a keen assessment of *Manhunt* 1954 July–Oct.

• **Vince Nowell, Sr.** dissects **Sol Cohen's** tactics to save *Amazing Stories*.

• **Richard Krauss** examines Charlie Chan's media empire, with special emphasis on Renown Publications' digest magazine.

• **Steve Carper** reports on the one, the only, Bronze Books and trailblazers **Luke Roberts** and **Jesse Lee Carter**.

• **Tom Brinkmann** exposes *The Creature from the Black Lagoon* with *The Seven Year Itch*.

• Fiction by **Robert Snashall** and **Joe Wehrle, Jr.**, with art by **Carolyn Cosgriff**.

• News updates from *Ellery Queen* and *F&SF*, to *Switchblade* and *EconoClash Review*, and everything in between—direct from their editors' lips

• Reviews of *Alfred Hitchcock's Mystery Magazine* May/June 2019 and *Broadswords & Blasters* No. 9.

• Over 100 digest magazine cover images, cartoons by **Bob Vojtko** and **Brian Buniak**, a poem by **Clark Dissmeyer**, first issue factoids, and more.

The Digest Enthusiast No. 10
160 pages $8.99 print, $2.99 digital.

Get your print copies from Bud's Art Books, DreamHaven Books, Mike Chomko Books, Barnes & Noble (online), eBay, or Amazon. *The Digest Enthusiast* is also available in digital format for Kindle and Magzter.

ECONO CLASH review # ONE

SOLDAN
McQUISTON
RUTHERFORD
MANDOLILLO
MEURDEREMANS
GRAVES
GARY
PLATT
PEREY
MINTER
TURNER III

EDITED BY:
J.D. GRAVES

QUALITY
CHEAP
THRILLS

ECONO CLASH review # TWO

Alec Cizak
Preston Lang
Oh Wish
Robert Petyo
Victoria Dalpe
C.A. Miller
James Harper
Beatrix M.G. Nielsen
Brandon Alexander
Tom Miller
James Harper
Joshua Hill

QUALITY
CHEAP
THRILLS

Edited By:
J.D. Graves

ECONO CLASH review #3

MAX SHERIDAN
MICHAEL BRACKEN
SARA DOBIE BAUER
RICK McQUISTON
KRISTEN BRAND
NICK SWEENEY
LEROY B. WUCHI
BRIAN JAMES LEWIS
CHRIS STANLEY
NICOLA LOMBARDI
JOE WESTHOUSE

QUALITY
CHEAP
THRILLS

EDITED BY: J.D. GRAVES

SPRING 2019

ECONO CLASH review #4

QUALITY
CHEAP
THRILLS

REX WEINER
A.B. PATTERSON
MARK SLADE
C.W. BLACKWELL
MATTHEW X. GOMEZ
JON ZELAZNY
HAILEY PIPER
J.S. ROGERS
ROBERT PETYO
J.L. BOEKESTEIN
HATEBREAKER

EDITED BY:
J.D. GRAVES

CIRSOVA™

Magazine of Thrilling Adventure and Daring Suspense
Issue #2 / Fall

Pawn to the Queen
by
Christine Lucas

The High Priest of Anubis must right a dreadful wrong!

*Chilling adventure of the ancient world from Christine Lucas
plus ten more tales of action, fantasy, horror and romance in the
Fall Cirsova Magazine of Thrilling Adventure and Daring Suspense!*

Available through Amazon, Barnes & Noble and wherever books are sold!

www.cirsova.wordpress.com

Hard-boiled pulp from the mean streets down under

PI Harry Kenmare

Sydney. Above - a beautiful harbour city. Below - sinful, seedy, and corrupt.
PI Harry Kenmare. A man who has lost everything. A man who is going to have his revenge.
He'll shatter the Establishment's hypocritical façades. And his way is far from pretty, unlike his women.

Reviewers' comments on the Harry stories...

"ballsy and literate, in the Chandler/Bruen style"
"sheer grittiness"
"humor and excitement"
"incredibly well written"
"not for prudes"
"raw, profane fiction"
"a private eye novel with real grit and drive"

From the pen of former detective sergeant A.B.Patterson

www.abpatterson.com.au

Gritty, brutal, sexy, noir - Australian-style

    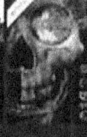   

       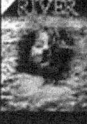

READ YOUR WAY TO MADNESS!

DEATH'S HEAD PRESS

www.deathsheadpress.com

FAHRENHEIT 13

AN IMPRINT OF FAHREHEIT PRESS

RISING FROM THE ASHES OF THE MUCH LOVED NUMBER
THIRTEEN PRESS - FAHRENHEIT 13 IS A NEW IMPRINT
FROM PUNK NOIR VETERANS FAHRENHEIT PRESS.

NOIR LEGEND CHRIS BLACK IS INSTALLED AS EDITOR
IN CHIEF AND IS ACCEPTING SUBMISSIONS NOW

F13NOIR@FAHRENHEIT-PRESS.COM

FAHRENHEIT 13 WILL RE-PUBLISHING ALL OF THE
ORIGINAL NUMBER THIRTEEN PRESS NOVELLAS
AS WELL AS COMMISSIONING AWESOME NEW
CRIME FICTION FROM ALL AROUND THE WORLD.

PULP ★ CRIME ★ NOIR

WWW.FAHRENHEIT-PRESS.COM

@FAHRENHEITPRESS   @F13NOIR

SWITCHBLADE

NOW AVAILABLE AT

DESCONTROL
PUNK SHOP
1725 E 7TH ST #C LOS ANGELES
OPEN EVERY DAY
12-8PM

SELL TRADE

BUY DESTROY

(IG) DESCONTROL_SHOP

CLOTHING • LEATHER • ACCESSORIES • RECORDS • TAPES

"*Lake County Incidents* is like the Winesburg, Ohio of the weird and wretched. Cizak's precise and simple prose proves the most horrifying thing an author can show readers is a mirror."
- Marc E. Fitch, author of *Paradise Burns*

MACABRE STORIES BY ALEC CIZAK

LAKE COUNTY INCIDENTS

ABC
GROUP DOCUMENTATION

Available Now

Author Bios & Acknowledgements

Eric Beetner is that writer you've heard about but never read. Then when you finally do you wonder why you waited so long. There are 20 of them so you'd better get started. Books like Rumrunners, All The Way Down and The Devil Doesn't Want Me. He also co-hosts the podcast *Writer Types* and the *Noir at the Bar* reading series in L.A.. He's been described as "The 21st Century's answer to Jim Thompson" (LitReactor) He's been nominated for three Anthony's, an ITW award, Shamus, Derringer and 5 Emmys. Seriously, what are you waiting for?
www.ericbeetner.com

Callum McSorley is a writer based in Aberdeenshire, Scotland. His short stories have been published, or are due to appear, in *Gutter Magazine, Typehouse Literary Magazine, Hardboiled (Dead Guns Press), Shoreline of Infinity,* and more. @CallumMcSorley

callummcsorley.com

John Moralee was born in England, where his crime, horror and science-fiction stories have been published in various magazines and anthologies, including *The Mammoth Book of Jack the Ripper Stories, Crimewave* and *The British Fantasy Society's official magazine* short fiction includes Warlock's Eye (*FunDead Publications*), Fools at the Feet of a Hanged Man

(*Dodging the Rain*), Special Service (*Longshot Island literary magazine*), Castrato (*Things in the Well*) and The Life Model (*Dark Rainbow).*

Mandi Jourdan graduated from SIUC with a BA in English/Creative Writing and a minor in Classics, and she is currently pursuing her MFA in Fiction. She is the author of the novels "Lacrimosa" (Adelaide Books) and "Veritas" (Adelaide Books) as well as "Shadows of the Mind" (Aphotic Realm), the short story collection set in the same world, among other publications. *The Shadows of the Mind* podcast based on her novel series is available on all major platforms. When not writing and listening to eighties rock, she spends time with her cats. Find her on Twitter (@MandiJourdan) or at **bloodandtalons.wordpress.com.**

Hugh Lessig is a career journalist who lives and works in the Hampton Roads region of Virginia, where he writes about the military, veterans issues and shipbuilding. His short stories and flash fiction have been published in *Thuglit, Shotgun Honey, Needle: A Magazine of Noir* and *Crime Factory.* His short story, "Last Exit Before Toll," will appear in the anthology *Mickey Finn: 21st Century Noir*, due out in 2020 from *Down and Out Books.*

Nick Kolakowski has appeared in *Shotgun Honey, ThugLit, Plots with Guns, Crime Syndicate Magazine, Mystery Tribune,* and various anthologies. I'm also the author of "A Brutal Bunch of Heartbroken Saps" and "Slaughterhouse Blues," two short novels from Shotgun Honey, and the upcoming "Boise Longpig Hunting Club" from *Down & Out Books.*

Alec Cizak is a writer from Indiana. His short stories have appeared in several journals and anthologies. His most recent novel, "Breaking Glass", is available from *ABC Group Documentation.* He is also the chief editor of the fiction journal *Pulp Modern*

Matthew X. Gomez maintains his web presence at mxgomez.wordpress.com as well as on twitter @mxgomez78. In addition to writing, he is one of the two conspirators running *BROADSWORDS & BLASTERS*, a new pulp magazine that debuted in 2017. Other work of his has appeared in *PULP MODERN, STORYHACK, SWITCHBLADE*, and in the anthologies *MIDNIGHT ABYSS* and *ALTERED STATES II.*

James Edward O'Brien's short fiction has appeared in *InterGalactic Medicine Show*, the *Tales of Blood and Squalor* anthology, and on the *Tales to Terrify* podcast.

Rob D. Smith is a is a struggling human attempting to write uncommon fiction in Louisville, KY. His work has appeared in *Apex Magazine*. He co-hosts a podcast that explores pop culture

story telling at
https://theabysmalbrutes.podbean.com/

Special Thanks to cover model Kiana
Gonzalez, *Skylight Books*, The Switchblade L.A.
Chapter, Rick West of *Battery Books*, Alec Cizak,
and Richard Krauss of *Pulp Modern*, for their
work on *Pulp Modern: Tech Noir,* and for their
continued support of *Switchblade*.

UNITED ARTISTS

SWITCHBLADE ISSUE ELEVEN
ALEC CIZAK J.D.GRAVES J.WILSKY
& MORE OCT 4

PARENTAL
ADVISORY
EXPLICIT CONTENT

ROBB T. WHITE

JIM WILSKY

DAVID RACHELS

MISHA BURNETT

SERENA JAYNE

GEORGE GARNET

BRIAN BEATTY

J.D. GRAVES

ALEC CIZAK

www.ingramcontent.com/pod-product-compliance
Lightning Source LLC
Chambersburg PA
CBHW070816120626
46556CB00002B/535